# I Remember Highway 80

ROBERT LACY

STEPHEN F. AUSTIN STATE UNIVERSITY PRESS

For more information:
Stephen F. Austin State University Press
P.O. Box 13007 SFA Station
Nacogdoches, Texas 75962
sfapress@sfasu.edu
www.sfasu.edu/sfapress

Book design: Jerri Bourrous
Cover design: Jerri Bourrous
Distributed by Texas A&M Consortium
www.tamupress.com

LIBRARY OF CONGRESS CATALOGING-IN-PUBLICATION DATA
Lacy, Robert
I Remember Highway 80/Robert Lacy

ISBN: 978-1-62288-151-2

FOR SUSAN

ACKNOWLEDGMENTS

A number of pieces in this book were originally published elsewhere and the author wishes to gratefully acknowledge that fact. "The Home Front, 1942-1945" first appeared in *The Sewanee Review*, as did "Our First Car," When Country Was Country," "Saturdays at the Paramount," and "Roy vs. Gene." "Football" and "A Gambol on the Golden Shore" first appeared in the *North Dakota Quarterly*, the latter in an earlier, fictionalized version titled "Three Hundred and Eighty-Six Jackrabbits." "A Yellow Rose" was first published (as "A Yellow Rose, in Texas)" in the hardbound anthology *Resurrecting Grace: Remembering Catholic Childhoods*, published by Beacon Press of Boston. "Up in the Ozarks" first appeared in the *South Dakota Review* and "Youth" first appeared in the *Chariton Review*.

The author would also like to aknowledge the help of his good friend Michael Fedo in reading, critiquing, and helping to improve these pieces over the past fifteen years.

# Table of Contents

# Introduction

Crockett is a small town in central East Texas, not far from Nacogdoches. It's where I was born, in 1936. My mother was a 22-year-old country girl from up in Wood County. Her name was Sarah Isabella Hughes, but people called her Sally Belle. My father was a strapping young man, well over six feet tall, named L.V. Lacy who had come over from Alabama to get in on the Great East Texas Oil Strike then centered around Kilgore. The initials L.V. stood for "Lester Vanandus." I have never been able to track down the origin of that second word and have no idea to what or whom it refers. "Vanandus." An oddity, and a mystery.

The year I was born, 1936, was one of the grimmest of the Great Depression. L.V. was working, when he could find work, as a truck driver, hauling logs to and from the lumber mills dotting that part of the piney woods of East Texas. I was born in Crockett but we didn't linger there. During the next few years we would live in places with such names as "Karo" and "Garrison" and "Diboll," lumber milling towns, mostly, with rows of little one-room cabins sitting on sawmill lots for the workers. It was tough, I'm told. Chaotic. Times were very hard. I can remember standing outside one of those worker cabins as a small child and watching through a window as the grownups inside played a new board game called *Monopoly* by the light of a kerosene lantern. Yes, *Monopoly*. In the depths of the Depression. By kerosene lantern-light. I remember that.

Possibly because of the times, and possibly because of other things, the marriage of L.V. and Sally Belle was

9

turbulent, was less than made in heaven. L.V. was on the road a lot, coming and going, appearing and disappearing. We were forever being snatched from one locale to another, mother and I. I have a dim memory of an evening—I must have been around three—when my father came into a room where my mother and another girl were standing together, talking. I remember him grabbing mother by the arm, tearing a button off her blouse in the process, and literally dragging her away from the other girl. Then, in my memory, the scene shifts and the three of us—mother, father and I—are together in the cab of his truck, and it is dark outside, and we are driving down a highway. There is a feeling of warmth and intimacy in the truck and I feel safe and comforted and very happy for a change. Like I say, I must have been about three at the time.

I also remember L.V. returning from a trip somewhere in his truck, and climbing down out of its cab and handing me a little clear-glass piggybank, within which a single nickel could be seen, and heard, rattling around. Oh, such a happy day!

L.V. was killed, though, when I was five. He died when the truck he and his younger brother Horace were riding in slid off a rain-slick road down near Conroe, Texas, and smacked into a big oak tree. This happened in the early spring of 1942, just weeks after the Japanese attack on Pearl Harbor. Horace was driving the truck. He survived. L.V. was pronounced dead at the scene, his skull crushed by the shifting lumber that came crashing through the truck cab's back window. Mother and he were already legally separated by this time, although I wouldn't learn this until years later, when mother finally told me. "It wasn't a good marriage, Bob," was all she would ever say on the subject.

I have in my possession an eight-by-ten photograph of my father and me. It's an enlargement of a smaller shot—I myself had it enlarged—and is therefore a little fuzzy around the edges. The photo is in black and white, color photography not yet being widespread. It shows L.V.

and me sitting on the front steps of a house somewhere, location unknown. It's a white frame house, though, and there's a street address in fairly big numerals on the wall behind us. "645," it says. So, apparently, we were living at "645 Somewhere" when the picture was taken. In it, L.V. is wearing his truck driver uniform of khaki pants and a khaki shirt, with epaulets. He is bareheaded and his full head of dark hair shows. He is wearing a pair of high-topped lace-up black shoes of the kind elderly men used to wear in those days, but the shoes look rather elegant on him. He has big feet. He's also wearing a pair of rimless glasses. He is a large man, wide shoulders, long legs. He has presence. There is no other word for it. In the picture at least, my father has presence. He has the look of a man who owns the space he occupies, and knows it. He also has a ring that looks to be made of Mexican silver on the ring finger of his left hand. A faintly dandyish touch, it seems to me now.

Seated beside him, up close, is a little towheaded tyke in striped overalls and dirty bare feet. That's me. I look to be, again, about three at the time. I've got my right hand gripped tight in the crook of his arm in a way that looks extremely possessive. (This is *my* daddy!) I appear to be holding on tight, even as I squint up into the bright sunlight for the camera.

L.V. was thirty-three when he died, the same age as Jesus. I wrote an essay about him which appeared in *The Sewanee Review* several years back. I called the essay "A Reason To Write," and its thesis was that writing is a way of leaving a record for those who come after us, and is therefore a worthwhile thing to do. I know precious little about my father because nobody—at least nobody I know of—kept a record of his life and experiences. I don't even know the origin of his middle name! Mother was always very reticent where he was concerned. It was difficult to draw her out. I don't blame her for this; there must have been pain involved in their time together. But it has left me bereft and longing where half of my heritage is concerned.

 

The pieces that follow were written over the course of the past fifteen years. They deal, for the most part, with the years following my father's untimely death, and if they have a central figure, other than the author, me, it is my mother. She is the heroine of these pieces, as you will see.

Mother always maintained that she had been born a hundred years too late. She felt she should have been a pioneer wife, out on the far frontier somewhere, breaking new ground with a hearty band of freshly arrived settlers. She used to tell me this, quite seriously. I think she pictured herself, dressed in gingham and a sun bonnet, standing by her man, a sturdy John Wayne type, no doubt, as he fended off hostile Comanches, perhaps even loading his spare Winchester for him as he took aim with the other one. She could have excelled at something like that, she felt quite certain.

She was a small woman, mother, standing only five, feet four in her stockinged feet and never in her life, except perhaps when she was carrying me, weighing more than a hundred and twenty pounds. But, as she used to tell me with a smile of shy pride, "I had a nice figure." She was also an impulsive woman. She would get wild ideas in her head, and she liked nothing better than acting on them, as you will see in the essay called "The Retrieval" in which she, surrendering no doubt to impulse, decides to drive fifteen hundred miles from Marshall, Texas, to the Marine Corps Recruit Depot in San Diego, California, to bring me back home for my initial 30-day leave following boot camp. Most people don't believe me when I tell them that. But it's true; it's what she did. My fellow marine recruits were astounded when she showed up out there, as were our drill instructors. As am I, even now, remembering it.

Mother was born in Peach, Texas, a little town in Wood County that no longer exists. She was one of six surviving children of Eddie Pogue and Claude McKinney Hughes.

Eddie Pogue, my grandmother, came from a family of early settlers in Wood County. She grew up in Quitman and was a childhood friend of the "Stinson girls," one of whom would eventually marry James S. Hogg, a future governor of Texas. Mother had three brothers and two sisters. She felt that her mother, Eddie, favored the three boys and gave them preferential treatment. She used to tell me that. She complained about having to get up "before dawn" to fix breakfast for her brothers. Her mother paid little attention to the girls, she felt. She bitterly resented this, and I was still hearing about it when I was in high school.

Claude Hughes, my grandfather, had been the postmaster at Peach. But when the railroad that had been the town's reason for existence got pulled up and carted away, the town quickly vanished with it. Claude was a sweet-natured man, according to all reports; all the Hughes men, mother's brothers, were (maybe because they had been so pampered by Eddie). Claude used to take me with him when he walked the lumberyard in Kilgore, where we were then living, marking with his yellow chalk the big pine logs stacked there row on row. He was marking them for disposition by the big circular saws in the sawmill: Grade A, suitable for lumber; Grade B, less suitable for lumber; and so on. We were all crowded together, three families of us, in a small house on the highway out south of Kilgore. Claude suffered from sleep apnea, though they didn't call it that back then; you could hear him snoring all over the house. It used to scare me. He sounded like a lion. He died of a heart attack, at 55, in the same year my father died in his truck accident: 1942. Not a good year for me.

During World War II we lived for a time in Houston, where mother worked in a shipyard. She was an "expediter," whatever that meant, and got her picture in *The Houston Chronicle* one day, illustrating a piece on women's contributions (as I remember it) to the war effort. I fell out of the top of a chinaberry tree in Houston, but walked away miraculously unhurt. I also had my tonsils out there. After the war we moved back up to Marshall, in East Texas, and roomed for a year with mother's older sister Marie and her family in a nice house in the town's east end. All of this is recounted in the essay called "The Home Front, 1942-1945" which appeared in *The Sewanee Review* in the fall of 2015. Aunt Marie was my favorite among mother's siblings. She was a good cook and had a lively sense of humor. I recall a night, when she and her family were living in Palestine, Texas, and mother and I were down there, visiting. The grownups began telling jokes for some reason, and the jokes soon turned bawdy. Marie's kids, my cousins, and I raced from grownup to grownup, wide-eyed and wide-eared, as the humor got bluer and bluer. It was a time when jokes based on imaginary book titles were all the rage, and Marie's contribution that evening, as I remember it, was "*A Hole in the Mattress* by Mister Completely." I was about nine at the time and thought that was hilarious, although I wasn't entirely sure I got it.

Mother also had a younger sister named Mary Jo. Mary Jo married a Wood County fellow with the last name of Meezles and had a son by him, but she left Meezles during World War II and ran off with a deserter from the U.S. Navy, a Mexican-American named Lawrence Torres. For years nobody knew where they were. They finally turned up out in San Bernardino, California, in the 1950's, living in a very poor neighborhood. Lawrence was working as a waiter in a hotel restaurant downtown. They had two young daughters and a young son; one of the daughters, I remember, was named Joanne. I visited Mary Jo and her new family once when I was stationed out at nearby Twentynine Palms in the marines. They fed me fried eggs for breakfast and urged me to put a hot picante sauce on them. It was how they ate their eggs. I did as they asked but thought the whole business far too exotic. Mary Jo and her brood don't figure in the pieces that follow, though, because the pieces are concerned with my growing up in East Texas, when they weren't around. Mother did keep in touch with her once she'd been located and was never judgmental where Mary Jo and her life choices were concerned, but I always sensed a certain sadness in her whenever the subject of Mary Jo came up.

Someone who does figure in several of the following pieces, however, is a young man I have called "Neil Pomeroy" in various things I have written about him over the years, both fiction and nonfiction. His actual name was Bob Bartlett. We first met in the third grade at Southside Elementary School in Marshall, and Bob became my best friend all the way through high school, although I could never be quite sure I was his. Bob had a lot of friends. He was naturally charismatic. Everyone was drawn to him. He was the captain of the football team, captain of the basketball team, Most Popular Boy, Boy Most Likely to Succeed, all of it. He seemed born to be young, though, and he didn't age well. Something went out of Bob in his middle thirties, some spark, and he was only a shadow of himself after that. He's the central figure in my hybrid memoir/essay called "Youth." Bob/Neil died suddenly, of a heart attack, at the age of fifty-one, some twenty years ago now, and the last few times I saw him before then he had grown heavy and pasty-faced and didn't appear to be a happy man. He seemed angry. I think he knew, or sensed, he had a bad heart. Life will have its way with us.

On a cheerier note, in the piece titled "A Gambol on the Golden Shore," which closes out the book, I recount a trip I took out to El Centro, California, in my senior year of high school with a couple of other boys, Bob/Neil not one of them, from Marshall. We made the trip, leaving town in the spring of that year, just before my scheduled high school graduation, because we had been reliably informed that a junior college out there was dying to get its hands on some genuine Texas football players. We were answering their call. That things didn't work out quite like we expected would end up being beside the point. It was an adventure, a heck of a trip, and great fun all around. This piece originally appeared as a short story in the *North Dakota Quarterly* back in 2002. At that time I called it "Three Hundred and Eighty-Six Jackrabbits" because of the astounding number of such silly, lop-eared creatures we encountered, dashing across the roadway in front of us, as we made our way out to California and back. Who could have imagined there were so many jackrabbits in this world? The piece was considerably longer in its earlier version, with lots of scenes and lots of dialog. But it was a true story then, although some of the scenes and much of the dialog were invented, and it's an even truer story now.

High school football was very much part of the culture in East Texas when I was growing up there. Whole towns gathered under the lights at local stadiums on Friday nights in the fall. I imagine they still do. Two of the pieces offered here deal with the phenomenon, the one called, fittingly enough, "Football" and the longish piece discussed above that I now call "A Gambol on the Golden Shore." It took me years to outgrow my fixation with football, and my wife might tell you, if you asked her, that I haven't fully outgrown it yet. All I can say in my defense is that Doak Walker and Bobby Layne, Kyle Rote and John David Crow were magical names when I was a boy growing up in East Texas, and as cultural heroes go they still seem to me better candidates for the role than most.

I worked in a drugstore in Marshall, off and on, beginning when I was fifteen. It brought me into contact with an interesting man named Bob Martin, the proprietor of the store. Bob was also the star of the minstrel show put on each year by the local Lions' Club and called, with no great effort at wit or originality, "The Lions' Loonies." Bob stuttered badly in his offstage, everyday life but never when he was up in front of a crowd as "Mister Interlocutor" for the Lions' Loonies. I always found that amazing. He and I used to go to a café in town after we closed the store for the day and to order and eat there large bowls of "wop salad." You'll have to read the piece ("Drugstore Days") to see what those were. Bob Martin was, as I say, an interesting man. And it was in his store that I first met Nell Rose Worley, an equally interesting woman and a world class seamstress (at least in her own mind), as you will see.

Mother converted to Catholicism when I was twelve, and took me with her. It worked for her, if not for me, and was the right thing for her to do. She found what she was looking for—comfort, certainty, an orderly view of things—in the church, and she made most of her latter day nonfamily friends there. They were people with distinctly un-East Texas-sounding names, such as Cacciopia, Maranto, and Dufresne. Mother's newfound Catholicism figures in several of the pieces included here, but most notably in "A Yellow Rose," in which I explore her relationship with a little Irish-born priest named Father Charles Gormley, who could sing like a Celtic angel. Father Gormley, who also tutored me in math, would turn out to be an important figure in both our lives. This piece was first published in an anthology called *Resurrecting Grace: Remembering Catholic Childhoods* put out by Beacon Press of Boston back in 2001.

Mother had found work as a "laboratory assistant" at a munitions factory outside Marshall during the last months of World War II, and after the war ended she was able to transfer the lab skills she had learned there to a small plant called Darco in the west end of Marshall, where her new job title became "laboratory technician." She would work at Darco for more than thirty years, through several changes of ownership. The building she worked in was called "DXL," which stood for "Darco Experimental Laboratory." I always thought that sounded pretty cool: my mother, the laboratory experimenter. Darco processed lignite coal from a mine out south of town, turning it into activated carbon for use in water filtration systems and in the manufacture of carbonated soft drinks. In the beginning it was filthy work. She would come home with her coveralls caked with raw lignite and with big raccoon-like rings around her eyes from where her safety goggles had been. She started at Darco at fifty cents an hour, working forty-eight hours a week, but by the time she retired at age sixty-five she was a full-fledged "junior" chemist despite never having gone to college. By then Darco had become owned by a big London-based multinational corporation called ICI, and they used to fly her to their other plant sites around the U.S. where she would instruct the locals on how best to "cook" the chemical formula for the purification product they were peddling. That's how good a chemist she had become.

In 1985, at the age of seventy-one, mother took it in her head to join the Peace Corps, which is apparently always in need of trained chemists to work among the villagers in out of the way places such as the African bush and the jungles of the Philippines. It was while she was in training in Puerto Rico for an overseas assignment that she began to feel weak and out of sorts and was eventually diagnosed by Peace Corps doctors as having stomach cancer. She didn't get to complete her Peace Corps training or to carry out her Peace Corps assignment, which I'm sure was a big disappointment to her. She died back at home in Marshall, with me at her side, on the last day of 1986.

In looking back over these pieces I find myself struck by how many of them deal with car travel. There are two trips all the way out to California and back, for instance, plus another one to Tucson, Arizona. And trips down into Mexico and up to Kansas City. Why all this mobility? I think it's probably because the 1950's, when much of what is recounted here was set, were a sort of Golden Age of the automobile in America. Gasoline was cheap (especially in oil-rich Texas), people were beginning to have money in their pockets after years of economic depression and world war, and even working widows, like my mother, were able to afford their own cars. (See my little essay "Our First Car".) The roads were good and getting better and a sense of optimism was abroad in the land. So why not travel? Why not visit new places? As that popular singer of the day Dinah Shore used to put it, in what was probably the most often-run TV commercial, ever, "See the U.S.A. in your Chevrolet!"

I have arranged these pieces more or less chronologically, beginning with "The Home Front: 1942-1945," when I was about five or six, and carrying on through until the time when I joined the marines, in 1955. (See "The Retrieval"). Mother and I lived in about a dozen different houses during that time, but I don't remember all of them. The ones in Marshall I do remember, and I try to account for them here. In a couple of the pieces—"Up in the Ozarks" and "Youth"—the dialog is largely invented because no one can remember what was said 60 years ago. But in all cases the events and the people involved are and were real. What I say happened, happened, with an occasional burnishing for the sake of story, and at least as I remember it.

# The Home Front, 1942-1945

World War II was good for us. In the months leading up to it, mother was working in a sawmill commissary in Kilgore for eleven dollars a week. But following the attack on Pearl Harbor word quickly reached East Texas that the shipyards down in Houston were hiring, and paying good money, and that there were plenty of jobs for all.

Mother and her younger brother, John Allen, decided to roll the dice. Within weeks our two families—mother and I; John Allen, his wife Doris, and their two kids, Roger and Gay—were installed in a small frame house on Common Street in a rundown section of Houston. The little house had two bedrooms: a small one for mother and me, and a larger one for Johnny and his brood. There was also a living room, bathroom, and kitchen. The kitchen came equipped with a stove and an icebox. Not a refrigerator, an icebox—for which an iceman had to deliver a big gray block of ice one or more times a week. I remember this icebox particularly well because Roger and I turned it over one night while wrestling on the kitchen floor. I remember the milk spilling out of it onto him and me, the general mess the icebox's contents made on the linoleum covered floor, and, most of all, the spanking we each got soon after the icebox had been placed upright again and the floor mopped up. I was six when this happened; Roger was five.

There were two big shipyards in Houston at the time. One was called simply Houston Shipyard and the other was called Brown Shipyard. Johnny went to work as a welder's helper at Houston Shipyard and mother went to work as an "expediter" at Brown. They were each paid about forty dollars a week as I remember it, a huge improvement over the prevailing wage back up in Kilgore. Brown Shipyard was a wartime spinoff of Brown & Root Construction, whose owners would become in later years big financial backers of Lyndon Johnson. I'm still not sure what an "expediter" was, but I think it had something to do with making sure all the various parts required in building a ship got to the right place at the right time and in a suitable number, something like that. They were making small, fast boats called destroyer escorts, or DE's, at Brown, and turning them out by the dozen. Somebody had to keep track of what was going on. And mother, with her high school education, became one of the ones who did. A photographer for *The Houston Chronicle* newspaper came out to the shipyard one afternoon and took a picture of her seated up on a stack of DE materials. She was holding a clipboard in one hand and a pencil in the other and appeared to be checking off items destined to become part of yet another DE. She looked perky and cute as could be—sort of a cross between "Rosie the Riveter" and a Hollywood glamour gal—perched up there in her coveralls, her hardhat pushed back on her head. We kept a copy of that picture around the house for years afterward, but finally misplaced it in one of our many moves. I wish I still had it.

Most of my memories of Houston are sketchy and rather dim. It was many years ago; I was only six. I remember that there were several large boarding houses across the street from us, and that they were two-story, frame, and in need of paint. I remember waiting out a hurricane in the front room of the little house on Common Street, watching roofing shingles being ripped off the boarding houses across the way and being frightened by both the high wind and heavy rain, and by the fireballs off the electricity transformers that went rolling gaily down the street. I remember getting hit in the head by a rock on a playground, but I don't remember who threw it, or why. I remember Roger, who had a quick temper, chasing me around the yard one day with a butcher knife in his hand. I remember falling out of a chinaberry tree in our backyard, plunging down through the leaves and branches for what seemed like a long time, but then being miraculously unhurt when I finally hit the ground. It was as if I were Captain Marvel or somebody. I simply stood up, brushed myself off, and went back to my play. I remember suffering something called a "stone bruise" on the heel of one of my feet, and then lying in bed with the stone-bruised foot elevated so as to alleviate the throbbing. I also remember that I had my tonsils taken out. And, oh yes, I remember having to eat lemon meringue pie until it was coming out my eye sockets because I had made too much of a fuss about wanting more than the piece mother had originally cut for me. It was her way of curbing my gluttonous behavior. It worked. Oh, lordy, did it work. I still can't think of lemon meringue pie, even today, without experiencing a rising in my gorge.

Mother enjoyed her time in Houston, I think. She liked being gainfully employed, and making good money, and I think she liked the workplace and the people she met there, people with different backgrounds from those one might meet up in East Texas. I have memories of her coming home to Common Street rather late some nights, after a party or some other kind of get-together. Maybe a date. Aunt Doris was there at home to look after me as well as her own two, so mother was relieved of worry on that score. She could go to a party if she liked. She could go out dancing. And I hope she did.

We might have stayed in Houston for the duration of the war if John Allen, despite his responsibilities as a husband and father, despite his working in an essential wartime industry, hadn't finally, in 1944, been drafted. When he reported for duty in the U.S. Army, we—his wife and children, his older sister and nephew (me)—packed our skimpy belongings and headed back to East Texas. Doris and her two moved in with her family, the Dobbses, in rural Wood County, and mother and I landed in Marshall, over in Harrison County, where she had gotten wind of another defense-industry job, as a laboratory assistant, at Longhorn Ordnance Works in nearby Karnack. Longhorn Ordnance Works made artillery shells and signal flares. Occasionally there would be an explosion out there. What this job paid I don't recall, but it was less than the Brown Shipyard wage, I'm pretty sure. We moved in with mother's older sister, Marie, and her husband, Mack Wheeler, and their three kids—Sue, Jerry, and Anne—there on Austin Street in Marshall, just a few doors away from the campus of East End Elementary School, which I would soon be attending. Uncle Mack had been able to avoid the draft, a state of affairs that made my cousin Jerry, his son, a tad defensive on the subject of wars and warfare. Mack was employed temporarily as a guard out at Longhorn Ordnance Works, where if memory serves me correctly he stood nightly guard duty up in a spotlight-equipped tower, making sure Nazi saboteurs never breached the gates of Longhorn Ordnance. Jerry used to brag to me that he stood those watches armed with a "luger," the luger being a German pistol that had achieved a certain *cachet* in those days because of its frequent brandishing by enemy officers and agents in the war movies of the period. I think Jerry was making this up in an effort to elevate uncle Mack's wartime status, but I never pressed him on it.

The Wheelers had a nice two-story house, so Mack must have been doing well financially. Before the war he had been a salesman for a wholesale grocer. He let us have a downstairs bedroom in the front of the house. I remember mother admonishing me about thinking I somehow had the run of the place. We were to stick to our bedroom as much as possible, she insisted, and not go clogging up the halls and passageways of the rest of the house, not go barging into other people's living space. I didn't take her too seriously, however, and remember spending much of my time upstairs with Jerry, who was a year older than me, making model airplanes with him in his room. We built a lot of model planes together, he and I, and had great fun doing it. If I close my eyes I can still see those flimsy little balsa-wood-and-tissue-paper aircraft we so painstakingly constructed with our X-acto knives, those Grumman Hellcats and Japanese Zeroes, those German Messerschmitts and P-51 Mustangs; I can still smell the intoxicating, room-filling aroma of Testor's airplane glue.

We also played "guns" a lot outside, Jerry and I. We would go see a movie like "Back to Bataan" or "Objective Burma" on Saturday at the Paramount Theater there in Marshall and would then come home and act it out again in the empty lot next door, which had a creek running through the back of it, the banks of which were good for ambush concealment and the like. I remember taking those make-believe combats very seriously. I had a helmet and a bayonet and a toy submachine gun, and Jerry and our other neighborhood playmates were similarly decked out. We rushed around, charged each other's positions, and died gracefully when shot. We fought the "Japs" when we'd seen a war movie set in the Pacific and the "Nazis" when we'd seen one set in North Africa or Europe. It was harder to get playmates to pretend to be Japs, I remember, than it was to get them to pretend to be Nazis. Incipient racism? No doubt. In the movies we saw, the Nazis looked like us, the Japanese didn't.

Interestingly, Jerry would eventually serve in the Army in the mid-fifties at the same time I was doing a hitch in the Marines. During his Army tour Jerry would find himself at one point aboard a troopship out in the Pacific near a little atoll called Eniwetok. He was there, along with other Army enlistees, to serve as guinea pig witnesses to the first ever detonation of a hydrogen bomb. It must have been quite a show because the experience profoundly affected

Jerry for the rest of his life. He became an ultra-pacifist and spent much of his future adulthood working for an anti-war publisher on the West Coast. When I last saw him, after I got out of the Marines, he was running a little take-out laundry shop in San Francisco and reading philosophy in the back room in his spare time. I never could get him to talk about Eniwetok.

It was for Christmas of 1944 that I got as a present from Santa a toy pinball machine. The machine was about the size of an old-fashioned washboard, as I remember it. It was glass-covered, had a spring-activated plunger and a number of marble-sized steel balls for launching at the various flippers and holes on its playboard. I was delighted with it. It was just about the nicest Christmas present I had ever received. I couldn't wait to take it outside and show it to the neighborhood kids on Austin Street. Among them was an older boy of about ten who took an immediate liking to my pinball machine; he simply couldn't keep his hands off it. He fired the plunger over and over, manipulated the flippers with the buttons on the side, and sent the steel balls zipping and careening all around the board. When he finally relinquished it, he rushed home to his house and came right back with a handful of cardboard cutout soldiers, which he then proceeded to try to convince me were a better gift than any old pinball machine. He was very persuasive and eventually he succeeded. I swapped him straight up: my pinball machine for his cardboard soldiers. Mother, when I told her what had happened, was irate. She wanted me to march down to the boy's house and demand that he give back my pinball machine. But I wouldn't do it. I was too humiliated. *How could I have been so stupid?* The older boy ended up keeping the pinball machine, while I satisfied myself, as best I could, with the cardboard soldiers. The boy would be two grades ahead of me a few years later in Marshall High School. He turned out to be inordinately good at getting his own way. By his mid-twenties he was

President Lyndon Johnson's press secretary. Until recently, he was something of a fixture on PBS television, where he could often be seen in full man-of-the-people mode, defending the downtrodden from the rich and powerful.

I don't remember VE Day, which quick Google research tells me was May 8, 1945, but I do remember VJ Day. Victory in Europe had been long anticipated after the Normandy landings and the liberation of Paris, and it came as something of an anti-climax. But victory over Japan was sudden, abrupt, brought about by the two atomic bombs dropped, days apart, on Hiroshima and Nagasaki. With the announcement of Japan's surrender on August 14, 1945, the huge national celebration began. It had been a long and costly war. I remember us kids on Austin Street marching up and down the sidewalk, banging on pots and pans with big kitchen spoons. People were honking horns, rushing out onto porches and lawns, waving American flags, shooting off firecrackers and cherry bombs—all of it. We kids fed on the general excitement and pounded ever harder on our pots and pans. VJ Day meant that John Allen would be coming home from the Pacific. It meant that mother's first cousin Waymon Blundell ("Aunt Madge's boy"), who had jumped with the 82nd Airborne at Normandy, would now not have to go to the Pacific and would be coming home too. It also meant, unfortunately, that Longhorn Ordnance would be ceasing production of shells and signal flares and would be laying off a lot of people, but that was something for another day.

It was a different time, World War II. People were nicer to each other back then. The pressure of danger from abroad had welded everyone into a seemingly close-knit group: one big American family. We all had something to be against together. It cleared the air. Made things easier to see and understand. The entertainment of the day was keyed to this sense of unity and common purpose. The songs, the movies, the books and plays all contributed. Mother liked the Andrews Sisters and Glenn Miller. Among movie actresses she favored Greer Garson and Irene Dunne, admiring them, I think, for their stoicism and grit in the characters they played. When Greer Garson up and married Buddy Fogelson, a Texas oilman, mother was taken aback. She hadn't realized people could do that: step right out of the movies into real life—in Texas! Her own social life in Marshall wasn't as rich as it had been down in Houston. There were fewer eligible men, fewer things to do. She became friends for a while with a woman whose husband had been blinded in a welding accident. His name was Robert Lee. I can still remember the glazed, otherworldly look in his ruined eyes. Robert Lee had a friend who mother went out with for a while, but the friend drank and his crowd was fairly rowdy. I didn't like the situation, and said so. I had grown used to having my mother to myself. My grandmother, mother's mother, was visiting us and she said I must understand and allow mother to see whomever she liked. But when I brought up the drinking, "Big Mama," as I called my grandmother, changed her stance and agreed with me. Mother quit seeing the friend. I wasn't yet ten at the time. When I think back on the episode, and my part in it, it is not without an amount of residual shame. What right did I have? Who did I think I was?

Well, I knew who I was. I was Sally Lacy's little boy, a third grader, a newly enrolled Cub Scout, a maker of some really quite nifty model airplanes, thank you, and a fierce upholder of proper standards of conduct—especially for others.

Still, World War II had ended and we had made it through. The experience had been good for mother, and because of that, good for me. In the labs at Longhorn Ordnance she had learned transferable skills that would enable her to find peacetime work at Darco, a local company that made activated charcoal for water purification uses from the low-grade lignite coal mined just outside Marshall. She would eventually work her way all the way up to full-fledged chemist at Darco, despite never having gone to college. With money saved from Longhorn Ordnance, and from living rent-free with the Wheelers, she was able to make a down payment on a house on Crockett Street there in the East End. There wouldn't be much in the way of furniture to put in it, no curtains for the windows or rugs for the floors, but it would be a house—the first—of our very own. I would be nine years old when we finally took possession of it, and mother would be a slightly less cute and perky thirty-one.

—for Roger Allen Hughes (1938-2013)

# A Yellow Rose

Mother converted to Catholicism when I was twelve and dragged me along with her. Just why she did so, I have never been sure. One of the women she worked with was Catholic, though, from an old German family there in Marshall, and I've always assumed that had something to do with it. Also, I think mother, as a widow, found comfort in the rituals of the Catholic liturgy—this was before Vatican II—and possibly a sense of community in being able to count herself among the band of "outsiders" who made up the congregation of St. Joseph's Church. This was in staunchly protestant East Texas, after all, and many of her fellow parishioners had such un-East Texas-sounding names as Maranto, Caccioppia, and Dufresne.

After my father died in a highway accident when I was five, we lived for a time with mother's people in Wood County. But, finally, wanting to be on her own, mother moved the two of us to Marshall, where, with the exception of an older sister who would herself soon be moving, we didn't know a soul. Mother found work at Darco, a lignite-processing plant on the edge of town. She worked in their lab, running samples on the product, a powdery, low-grade form of coal used as a purifying agent in syrups, soft drinks and the like. In the beginning it was filthy work. She would come home in the evenings with her coveralls caked stiff with lignite and big, round, raccoon-like rings around her eyes where her safety goggles had been. But Darco was where she met Kathleen Resch, the woman from the German family, which led to her joining the Catholic Church.

29

The head pastor of St. Joseph's Parish in those days was a magnificent old priest named Father Meier. A notoriously soft touch for vagrants and other strangers passing through, he could nonetheless be brutally frank in his assessments of human frailty. The church maintained a flophouse for down-and-outers across the street from its side entrance. Told one day that the current occupants had managed to clog up the plumbing yet again, and asked what to do about it, he supposedly replied, "Ach, let 'em shit on the floor."

St. Joseph's was a very poor parish, even by the standards of hard-scrabble East Texas. The congregation, in addition to being small, included few of the town's professional people, or others likely to be generous when the collection plate came around. This forced Father Meier to exercise ingenuity in the hiring of his assistant pastors. What he did was to recruit them from Via Coeli (church Latin for "Way to Heaven"), the notorious sanctuary and drying-out facility for "troubled priests" out in northern New Mexico.

During my years as a member of St. Joseph's we must have had half a dozen of these wounded souls serving the parish at one time or another. They were without exception able, intelligent, *interesting* men. Well-educated and often well-traveled, they brought to Marshall a worldliness we weren't accustomed to. Of course, some of them brought a little too much worldliness—that had been their problem.

There was the priest I will call Father Claybaugh, for instance. Compact, curly-headed and red of face, he was a real dynamo when it came to organizing men's retreats and fundraising spaghetti dinners. He also delivered such eloquent Sunday sermons that Father Meier, whose task it ordinarily was, would often let him celebrate the high, ten o'clock mass in his stead. Father Claybaugh lasted with us nearly three years, his tenure coming to an end only after he locked himself into the top floor of the rectory one rainy Easter weekend and proceeded to drink two fifths of whisky and a whole case of beer.

Then there was Father Raekemper, the handyman. There was hardly anything Father Raekemper couldn't fix. He replaced all the hinges on the rectory doors and all the window screens at the convent school. He also rebuilt the boiler in the church basement and fine-tuned Father Meier's old car until it was the smoothest running '49 Packard in town. But then one night he jimmied his own lock off the sacristy door and got into the communion wine. We never saw him again after that.

And finally there was Father Gormley. He was my favorite. Born in County Cavan, Ireland, he had come over to this country as a teenager and had gone to school, on a City of New York Scholarship, as I remember it, at Fordham. Small-boned and sprightly, and with a shock of unruly black hair, he had a lovely tenor voice and a way of speaking to you that made everything he said sound musical. All we were told about him when he arrived, in the wake of Father Raekemper's departure, was that drink was not his problem.

Mother had been just twenty-seven when she was widowed, but she never remarried. Partly this was due, I think, to her unhappy experience the first time around— my father had apparently been something of a rambler— but partly, too, I think, it was due to mother's personality. She was fiercely independent, for one thing, and the same contrarian streak that had led her to join the Catholic Church in the midst of all those Baptists also made it hard for her to get along with people generally. Mother chose her friends carefully. The reason she liked Kathleen Resch, she told me once, was that "she's as mean as I am."

Not that mother didn't go out with other men while I was growing up; she did. I remember one I especially liked. He was an insurance agent there in town and had something to do with the Texas A&M Athletic Department, as a football recruiter or scout or something, and I can recall the two of them going away on a train for a weekend in Dallas one year at the time of the Cotton Bowl. He was a big, cheerful man who seemed to like me, and I had no trouble at all in picturing him as a daddy. But nothing ever came of it.

She also dated for a time, just as I was entering junior high school, a gentleman named Manoogian who had come to town to manage the local overall factory. I didn't much care for him, could never get used to the smell of his cigars and the sound of his loud, cocksure laughter. And when he ultimately threw mother over for his twenty-two-year-old secretary, I figured it was just as well. "Bobby Manoogian" was not a name I cared to cart around town anyway.

"Don't cry, mama," I can remember telling her. "At least we won't have those cigars lying around the house anymore."

This was the period when mother was converting to Catholicism, and we used to spend    a lot of time, she and I, at the home of Kathleen Resch. Unmarried, and a confirmed spinster, Kathleen lived with her family in a large, two-story stone house there on the square in Marshall. Her mother's name had been Umdenstock and that word was worked into the wrought iron gate out front of the premises. The Umdenstocks were among the earliest settlers in Marshall, I was told; their house had been built by slaves. On the mantle in the front room was a baroque gold clock, under glass, with a plaque on it commemorating the Louisiana Purchase.

All the priests used to hang out at the Resch house. There was usually plenty to eat there (and to drink too, now that I think of it). Lots of penny-ante poker hands got dealt around the big black table in the Resch's dining room, amid lots of cries of "You're bluffing, Father Claybaugh!" and "Read 'em and weep, Kathleen!"

There was an upright piano in the front room, and most evenings would end with all present grouped around it, singing. This was when Father Gormley would shine. He really did have a fine tenor voice; a bit thin on the highest notes maybe, but filled with feeling, always, and purer than spring rain on the rest. "Danny Boy" was one of his standards, of course, but he also sang "Kathleen Mavourneen," in honor of our hostess; "My Love Is from the Far Countree" (a James Joyce favorite I would later learn in college); and even, from time to time, "The Yellow Rose of Texas," because, as he said, he liked "the lilt of it."

Mother, who was tone deaf and couldn't carry a tune in a peach basket, would usually hang back during these group singings. But I can remember seeing her more than once with her eyes shut and her shoulders swaying as Father Gormley moved from octave to octave and back again on one of his ballads. His voice had that effect on people.

Although undersized and comically thin, I was doing my best at this time to excel at the game of football, it being so much a part of East Texas culture. I had tried out for and finally made the junior high school team as a ninth-grader, and as I entered high school, taller now but still a bit lean in the shanks, I continued to chase after gridiron glory. So much so that my grades had begun to suffer.

Into this breach stepped Father Gormley. When it wasn't occupied with cards and poker chips, he turned the Resch's dinner table into a study hall for me. And while others went about their socializing all around us, he put me through my academic paces. Math and science were my weakest subjects, and these turned out to be particular strengths of his. He used to drill me endlessly on geometry theorems and the basic algebra equations.

"You may be grand at kickin' a ball around, Bobby," he'd say, "but you'll need to know how to square your hypotenoose."

Mother and I were living in the Pinecrest Addition at the time, and he began appearing at our doorstep occasionally on weekends, to check up, he said, on my studies. "As I was in the neighborhood," he'd announce, "I figured I might as well flush out any lurking scholars." (He pronounced it "loorking".)

Mother would invite him into our little living room, ask him if he'd like some iced tea or coffee, and then leave the two of us to my homework as she went about her weekend chores of scrubbing the kitchen and bathroom. He must have stopped by half a dozen times like this over the course of several months.

And then one rainy autumn afternoon I came home early from football practice, in the middle of the week, to find him sitting there in the living room with mother.

"Why, there's the auld fella now!" he said, jumping up from the sofa as I walked in. "We've been waitin' for ye! Your mother tells me you're becomin' a dab hand at the algebra!"

Mother had risen from the sofa too. "Well!" she said. "You're home a little early, aren't you? I thought you had a scrimmage today."

"The field's all soggy," I said. "Coach sent us home."

"Too wet to plow, is it?" Father Gormley said.

"Yes, sir," I said. "Or anything else."

"Well!" mother said again. "Let's get you some supper fixed! Charles, uh, Father Gormley, was just leaving." She turned to him. "Weren't you, father?"

"Indeed, indeed," Father Gormley said. "I'd best be on my way. Father Meier will be wantin' his Packard back."

"Don't let me run you off," I said. "I'll just go make myself a sandwich."

"No, no, it's time to go," he said. "It's time to go. Belle will see me to the door."

My mother's name was Sally Belle. Some people called her Sally, some called her Belle. I've always thought it was the prettiest name imaginable. At this time she would've been in her late thirties and still a handsome woman. She saw Father Gormley to the door.

In the weeks and months that followed I never came home to find them on the sofa again, but I did overhear mother on the phone a time or two when she didn't seem to want to be overheard. Once, I'm fairly certain I heard her call her phonemate "Charlie."

But then one day toward Christmas of that year—funny how these things always seemed to happen around the church's high holidays—Father Gormley was no longer there. Suddenly, overnight, he was gone. Just like Father Claybaugh. Just like Father Raekemper. And there was never any official explanation. It was simply a matter of now you see him, now you don't.

We missed Father Gormley around the piano at the Resch's, and at the poker table. And, forced to confront alone that spring the sorrowful mysteries of trigonometry, I could have used him at the coffee table in our living room. But in the aftermath of his sudden disappearance nobody seemed to want to talk about where he'd gone, or why. It was as if a conspiracy of silence had enveloped St. Joseph's Parish, a great circling of the wagons, as it were, as our little Catholic community sought to cut its losses, conceal its casualties from the wider view.

I myself came close to bringing it up only once, one Sunday morning as mother and I were on our way to mass. Something had caused me to remember the missing priest, and I turned to mother and said, "Mama, I was wondering. What do you suppose ever happened to Father Gor—"

But that was as far as I got. We were in our little Chevrolet coupe, bought used the year before, the first car we'd ever owned. I was driving, and the look in mother's eyes told me to drop the subject, right there. So I did.

This all happened in my junior year in high school. Gradually, we forgot about Father Gormley. He was just another wayfarer, after all, another cut-rate priest Father Meier had lured down out of the hills of New Mexico. I managed to master trig on my own, and others arrived to fill out the poker games around the Resch's table. No one could be found to hit the high notes on "Danny Boy," though, or impart the proper lilt to "The Yellow Rose of Texas."

I never saw Father Gormley again—not face to face anyway. But something did happen a couple of years later that I've turned over in my mind a few times since. In the fall of that year, having finally come into my size, I had gone off up to Paris Junior College, in the north central part of the state, on a football scholarship. Paris is about a hundred miles from Marshall, and I used to hitchhike home on weekends with a suitcase full of dirty shirts and underwear for mother to wash.

One Friday evening my ride let me off down at the far end of our street, and as I was making my way up toward the house, suitcase in hand, I saw someone come hurrying out our front door, climb into the town's lone taxi, and leave. It was a man. He was about Father Gormley's size, and he moved with the peculiar rolling gait the little priest had. But the light wasn't good, and I couldn't see his face, and, besides, this fellow was wearing layman's clothes: some light-colored slacks and a sweater.

Was it him? I didn't know then; I don't know now. Something told me not to bring it up with mother, though. So I went on in the house, dumped my dirty clothes on her, and never did.

Mother is dead now. She succumbed to cancer some years ago. Her life was not a happy one. Through hard work and perserverance she finally achieved the financial security she had always longed for and her retirement years were well provided for. But she was alone, as she had been so much of her adult life, and she was lonely. She used to call me on the telephone late at night wherever I was— in the Marines, at college, or in one of the little university towns where I used to teach—and I could tell by the slur in her voice, usually, that she'd been drinking.

She died a devout Roman Catholic and was given the last rites and traditional burial honors of the Church. There was a funeral mass for her in St. Joseph's chapel. I had flown down from Minneapolis, which is where I live these days, to be with her in her final weeks. It rained the day of the funeral—hard, cold, driving—and the priest who presided at the gravesite, a new one I had never met, wore a quilted parka over his cassock and cowboy boots, I happened to notice, underneath it. He was a large, heavyset man, a bit wild eyed, and though Father Meier himself was long dead by then, I found myself wondering, *Via Coeli?*

In going through mother's belongings afterwards, preparatory to the estate sale that would liquidate most of them, I found in a trunk, among a lot of other stuff, some photographs I'd never seen before. They were in a big manila envelope, and most of them were of a fairly routine sort: pictures of family, of fellow workers out at Darco, of friends, and dogs, and other people's grandchildren. But one of them wasn't routine at all. It was a picture of mother and Father Gormley that looked to have been taken about twenty-five years earlier. It showed the two of them seated side by side on a picnic table at a park somewhere. There were other people in the background, but in the picture mother and Father Gormley were very much apart from them, and very much together. They were smiling at the camera almost impishly and the look on their faces was identical. The look said, "Yes, this is us, together, and we are having *fun*." There was such a suggestion of intimacy to the whole thing that it made me wonder who had taken the picture, Kathleen Resch?

Also in the manila envelope, protected within a little glassine envelope of its own, was a flower stem with a crisp brown leaf still attached to it. Smashed together at the bottom of the envelope were half a dozen brown petals and a white business card. The card carried the logo of an air conditioning firm in Silver Spring, Maryland, but the name on it read, "Charles A. Gormley, S.J." And underneath that were a Maryland address and two telephone numbers: the original number, with a line through it, and another number that had been penciled in under that.

I have saved the picture, but not the card, and not the flower. I had no desire then, at that late date, to try to contact the giver. And I certainly have no wish now, at this even later date, to do so. I assume Father Gormley is long dead too. If he's not, he's a very old man. I do take the picture out from time to time and look at it. It's such a happy shot, and such a pleasant way to remember mother.

Did anything *untoward* ever happen between her and Father Gormley? I don't know, of course, and I have no real interest in finding out. They're both gone, and I've long since drifted away from the church, so what could it possibly matter? Whenever the question occurs to me, though, and I confess it does occasionally, I always find myself hoping so.

# I Remember Highway 80

This is a hymn to a highway. Specifically, the late, great U.S. Highway 80, which used to run through Marshall, Texas, my hometown. It was done in by progress, by our continuing national quest for speed and bigness and the next new thing.

In days gone by it began in Savannah, Georgia, and ran all the way—some 2,726 miles later—to San Diego, California, on the sparkling Pacific. It was at the time the main east-west route across the country, and one of the first of the nation's numbered highways. Created by federal fiat in 1926, it retraced for much of its route what had been the old "Dixie Overland Highway," swapping the red clay mud of Georgia and Alabama for the blowing sands of Texas and New Mexico as it made its way west.

By the time it came into my life in the 1940s and 50s (or rather, I suppose, I came into its) it was a sleek, four-lane blacktop running smack through the throbbing heart of Marshall. It entered from the east through a leafy, upscale section of town known as Victory Drive and became, once it reached the town proper, "Grand Avenue," where, in such guise, it skirted the northern edge of the business district, past the Sears store, past the Piggly Wiggly supermarket, past the VA Hospital and Bishop College, on its way out to West End and the fabled Central East Texas Fairgrounds before, just past there, becoming Highway 80 again.

It's impossible to overstate what Highway 80 meant to Marshall in those days. It was the town's lifeblood. Sitting athwart this main east-west axis of commercial, vacation and personal travel gave Marshall constant, day and night, access to the wider world beyond. It gifted us with a daily infusion of higher octane energy than the local environment could ever hope to provide. There was a Dairy Queen on Grand Avenue, just down from St. Joseph's Catholic Church, where any day of the week one might see pull in for a quick chocolate malt or pineapple sundae cars with license plates from all over the continent. I remember seeing my first New York state license plate at that Dairy Queen one afternoon when I was about thirteen. It was a deep blue in color with orange numbering and letters, as I recall. "New York" it said across the top of the plate, and below the numbers, across the bottom, "The Empire State." *Wow*, I thought. *The Empire State. That's pretty neat. That's even better than the Lone Star State.*

Ernest Hemingway used to drive cross country from Key West, Florida, to Idaho and Wyoming in the days when he was married to first Pauline Pfeiffer and then Martha Gellhorn. He liked driving and he would no doubt have come through Marshall a time or two on his way west. His car of choice in those days, according to biographers, was a big black Buick. It would have been packed with his wife and three kids and maybe a few of his twenty-six cats. Did they ever stop at the Dairy Queen on Grand Avenue? I'm betting that they did. And it was just my bad luck to have missed them. I used to see all sorts of exotic passers-through at that Dairy Queen. Just the sight of them and their differently colored, otherworldly license plates would fire my imagination for days afterward.

Shreveport, Louisiana, sits forty miles due east of Marshall on Highway 80. Shreveport was, and is, a big town, second largest in the state after New Orleans. "The Louisiana Hayride," a popular Saturday night radio show patterned on "The Grand Ol' Opry" emanated from there in the 50's and captured a rapt audience all over East Texas. Elvis Presley played "The Louisiana Hayride." So did Hank

Williams. And Webb Pierce. And Johnny Cash. I used to go to bed on Saturday nights with "Your Cheatin' Heart" and "That's All Right, Mama" still ringing in my ears.

Midway between Shreveport and Marshall on Highway 80, and sitting right on the Louisiana-Texas line, was the little town of Waskom, population at that time about one thousand. Louisiana was still busy paying off the bonds for all the bridges Governor Huey P. Long had built back in the 30's and there used to be a sign on the eastern edge of Waskom saying "Leaving the State of Texas, Entering the State of Taxes." I don't know who put it there but it stayed up for a long time. Waskom was also the birthplace of Huddy Ledbetter, better known to the world at large as "Leadbelly," the great blues musician, but Huddy didn't spend much time there, preferring the faster pace of Houston when he wasn't enduring the much slower pace inside Louisiana's Angola State Prison.

Both Marshall and Waskom were in Harrison County, which in those days was "dry," meaning that you couldn't buy beer or liquor there. Shreveport, on the other hand, was "wet," and the legal drinking age in Louisiana was only eighteen, which guaranteed a whole lot of eastbound traffic out of Marshall, especially on a Saturday night. Twenty miles *west* of Marshall on Highway 80 sat the town of Longview, Texas. It was in Gregg County, which was also wet and which boasted a number of popular honky tonks such as Mattie's Reo Palm Isle, out on the highway between Longview and Kilgore. Big touring bands played the Reo Palm Isle, among them Bob Wills and His Texas Playboys. Packed cars not headed toward Shreveport, on Highway 80, on Saturday nights were likely on their way west, on Highway 80, toward Longview. For a boy growing up in Marshall it was sort of like living between Sodom and Gomorrah, only more fun.

Bonnie and Clyde were ambushed and killed just east of Shreveport on a little country road off Highway 80. This was in May of 1934, though, before my time. They were shot to tatters by legendary Texas Ranger Frank Hamer and several of his Ranger colleagues, using Browning automatic rifles (BARs) of the kind I would be introduced to some years later in the Marines. The coroner counted almost a hundred bullet holes  in the two bodies, making them so leaky the embalmer at the funeral home in Arcadia, Louisiana, had trouble keeping his fluid in them. Both Bonnie (Parker) and Clyde (Barrow) had grown up in and around greater Dallas in extremely spotty circumstances. It was the era of the Great Depression after all. They were glamorized by the Arthur Penn movie in the late 60's, starring the beautiful Faye Dunaway as an idealized "Bonnie" and the handsome Warren Beatty as an equally idealized "Clyde," but, really, they were just poor white trash and not very good to look at, to boot. Bonnie was twenty-three when she died. Clyde was twenty-five.

Dallas was 150 miles west of Marshall on Highway 80, a three hour drive unless the traffic turned bad, which, during State Fair time, it often did. My favorite memories of Dallas have to do with certain Saturday mornings in late fall when I was a high school football player. We played our games on Friday nights, and if we won somebody's father would often drive a carload of us to Dallas on Saturday to watch a bigtime college game that afternoon in the Cotton Bowl: SMU versus TCU maybe, or Texas versus Oklahoma. I can still see us prancing around outside the Cotton Bowl in our high school letterjackets, sizing up the boys from other towns, also there in their letterjackets to see the game. (I have written about this in a piece called "Football," which also appears in these pages.) Oh, what a thrill it was. And driving back home to Marshall after the game, passing or being passed by other cars on Highway 80, cars similarly filled with boys like us, honking the horn, waving, making "Hook 'em Horns!" or "Gig 'em Aggies!" signs out the window with our fore and pinkie fingers. What fun.

Highway 80 acts as something of a constant throughout this book, as you, reader, will be bound to notice sooner or later. It figures in one reminiscence after another. It's the route taken west by mother and me on our trip to Tucson, Arizona, in the piece called "Our First Car," and the route that brings us back home again to East Texas. It provides the pathway out to California and back in two other pieces, "The Retrieval" and "A Gambol on the Golden Shore." And it's the locus for the big motel in Longview featuring the Olympic-sized swimming pool that my friend Neil Pomeroy and I take our early-morning dip in on the way back home to Marshall in "Youth."

Like I say, a constant. When I was a boy growing up in East Texas there was no getting away from Highway 80. And no wanting to. It was a dominant factor in our lives. It figured in just about everything we did. It was our gateway to the world.

But nothing lasts forever, does it? Not youth. Not good times. Not even Highway 80. It was during the Eisenhower Administration that Congress passed, in 1956, something called the National Defense Highway Act. Putting the word "Defense" in the title like that assured the bill's passage in those early years of the Cold War. The National Defense Highway Act is what ultimately gave us, after the expenditure of God's own amount of federal tax money, the present interstate highway system, our own national Autobahn, every bit as grandiose as anything conceived by Albert Speer and his buddy Adolph Hitler. Part of the interstate highway system, Interstate 20, passes some twelve miles south of Marshall these days. It has succeeded by now in sapping most of the vitality from the town and it sounded, when finally completed in 1967, a definitive death knell for Highway 80. Each year more businesses pack up and move out to the Interstate 20 exits to be where the traffic is, leaving the former downtown "business district" of Marshall, with its quaint courthouse square and its brick streets, ever more empty and forlorn. Highway 80 is today no longer a main-traveled road, merely a farm-to-market afterthought for all the little dying towns it still straggles through. It also no longer traverses the country from sea to shining sea. As a designated route it officially ceases now just west of Fort Worth.

The interstate highway system, as impressive as it is, as time-saving and efficient as it may be, has done more to destroy smalltown America than anything else one could care to name. In bypassing them it has hung the Marshalls and Waskoms of this country out to dry, leaving them stranded in the middle of nowhere, with no future and no hope. By replacing them with those endlessly repetitious commercial clusters now found clinging barnacle-like to interstate exits all across this country it has introduced a numbing sameness into our national life and reduced car travel, which used to be adventurous, used to be *fun*, to nonstop boredom. And it has given rise to such grim little jokelets as:

"Where you from?"

"New Jersey."

"Oh, really? Which exit?"

On moonless nights, when the wind is right, we allow ourselves to call this progress.

## Our First Car

I was fifteen when we got our first car. The year was 1952 and the car was an off-white 1950 Chevrolet coupe, purchased used from a fellow who worked with mother out at the Darco lab. It had two doors and nappy upholstery, plus a working radio and a working heater. Neither mother nor I knew how to drive, so those first weeks of car ownership were tricky and not without peril. We had to enlist the help of a next door neighbor girl in getting us started. She would drive us out to a deserted country road and sit there in the front seat with us as we fought through the intricacies and coordination challenges of stick shifting and clutch-and-brake manipulation. She was just a teenager herself, and I took a fair amount of ribbing in the hallways at school for subjecting myself to her tutelage. But we couldn't have done it without her.

I remember the first day I drove the car to school. I was so full of myself, so proud. Lots of kids took cars to school, even in those days, even in comparatively hardscrabble Marshall, Texas. But this was the first time for me and I was intent on making the most of it. Things went fine until the noon lunch break when I piled three friends into the Chevy for a quick run to the Dairy Queen over on Grand Avenue. Now that I had wheels I could eat anywhere I wanted to. No more cafeteria food for me! I pulled away from the curb okay, and managed to shift into second gear to gain a little speed, but then somebody said something to me from the backseat and for some reason this caused me to slam on the brakes, right there in the middle of the street.

Unfortunately, there was a boy named Lyle Honeycutt on his motorcycle close behind us, and when I stopped suddenly like that he hit the rear of the car with such force that it broke the back bumper and sent Lyle over his handlebars and up onto the trunk of the Chevy. Kids were swarming out of the school building at the time and lots of them saw it. Luckily, Lyle wasn't hurt too badly, just a few bruises, but the car's bumper was a mess and my lack of driving skill had been exposed for all to see. It took me weeks to live the episode down and, needless to say, mother, when she saw the busted bumper, was not pleased.

Having the car made a big difference in our lives, though. It meant that we no longer had to rely on the town's few rickety public buses and its even fewer—I think there were a total of two—public taxis. Mother was a widow, and had been for more than ten years by this time. There were just the two of us. We had moved to Marshall after the war and she had taken a job as a lab technician at Darco, a small plant on the west side of town that processed lignite, a soft powdery form of coal, into "activated charcoal" for use in water filtration systems. Now that we had our own car, it became my job to drive mother to work each morning before going on to school and to pick her up each afternoon after work, except on days when I had football practice. Then she would make other arrangements.

Mother was fiercely independent. Her marriage to my father, a footloose Alabaman, had been a mistake. When he died in a highway accident they were already legally separated. She had lots of family in Wood and Gregg counties, but she'd moved the two of us to Marshall, in Harrison County, to get away from them. She intended to raise me on her own, she said, away from their interference. That was what she said. But she had been shamed, I think, by the way her marriage turned out, and she was still smarting from it. She didn't want her brothers, and especially their wives, throwing it up to her. She couldn't stand that. So we'd come to Marshall to make ourselves a life there.

Being a working widow in the 1950s was tough. The nation wasn't nearly so enlightened back then. Labor laws, particularly in Texas, were medieval. A woman alone faced job discrimination, poor pay, and very little chance for advancement. Mother started at Darco in 1946 at fifty cents an hour, working forty-eight hours a week. By the time I reached high school she was making more than that, but not a great deal more. We used to move from house to house as mortgage rates rose and fell, taking advantage of any little equity accumulation from increase in property value: a couple of hundred dollars here, a couple of hundred dollars there.

Petty humiliations were part of the package too. A woman without a man to protect her was seen by some as fair game. I remember once when, returning to Marshall by Trailways bus from a visit to Wood County, we engaged the lone cab at the bus depot to take us home. Instead of doing so, however, the cabbie circled the courthouse square and picked up another couple, a man and a woman, and then proceeded to take them to *their* destination, which was all the way out on the opposite side of town from where we lived, before driving us on home. Mother was outraged. She was beside herself. I must have been about nine at the time, and I can still see the hurt and anger in her face.

"You son of a bitch!" she shouted at the cabbie—she who never, ever swore—after he'd let the other couple out. "We were first! We were first!"

And I can still remember the cabbie's reply. Mother was pounding on his shoulders with her fists by now from the backseat, and he turned around and looked at her with a self-satisfied smirk.

"It's a free little country, lady," he said. "It's a free little country."

Having our own car meant she no longer had to put up with that kind of thing.

*

We had bought the car in the fall of that year, and by spring mother was planning a trip. We had some friends named Maranto whom we had met through St. Joseph's Catholic Church in Marshall. The Marantos were a large, lively Italian-American family who ran a grocery store across the street from the campus of Wiley College, a black institution of higher learning there in town. The eldest Maranto daughter, Sophie, was almost mother's age. She had recently moved with her new husband to Tucson, Arizona, and mother thought it would be a great idea, once school was out, for us to go visit them. So plans were made. The Marantos had another daughter, Lucia, their youngest, who was due to enter a convent in the fall, and Lucia, it was decided, would go along with us, to keep mother company, and as a final fling for herself before taking the veil.

We pulled out of Marshall on a fine June morning, heading west. There was no interstate system in those days and we made our way town by town on U.S. Highway 80. Tucson was some twelve hundred miles away. We did fine, with me driving, through East Texas, then Dallas, then Fort Worth, and finally out onto the great, arid plains of West Texas, the so-called *Llano Estacado*. The Chevy's little six-cylinder engine seemed to be performing about as well as any six-cylinder engine could. The day had turned hot, though, and with no air conditioning to keep us cool we had rolled down all the windows. I wanted to play the radio but mother decided we could do without it.

We spent the night in a tourist court in Abilene, the particulars of which I don't recall, then hit the road "bright and early" the next morning. The day got hot again in a hurry, the West Texas sun just blistering down. Sweetwater, Big Spring, Midland and Odessa came and went, with me driving again. It was on a long upward, though not terribly steep, incline somewhere west of Pecos that our luck ran out. I had kept an eye on the gauges as I drove and nothing seemed amiss, but suddenly there came a loud banging from under the hood of the car and, just like that, the engine stopped. Confounded, I pulled off onto the shoulder of the highway and coasted to a stop. Steam was rising from under the hood. I got out and looked beneath the car. I could see drips of oil puddling on the roadside gravel. There was a smell of burnt metal.

All of this was more than fifty years ago, so some of the details are hazy in my mind. Just how we got ourselves to the big truckstop-style service station out there in the middle of nowhere, I no longer recall. But we did get ourselves to it. Only to learn that the nearest auto mechanic was some forty miles away, in Van Horn. How we got to Van Horn is unclear to me now too, but I assume that either someone at the truckstop towed us or that someone from Van Horn came out and did so.

At any rate, we ended up spending three days in tiny Van Horn, Texas, while the lone mechanic there worked on our car. We had "thrown a rod," meaning a piston rod; it had gone through the engine block and come to rest in the oil pan. The engine was going to have to be rebuilt. Parts would need to be bussed over from El Paso. It was going to take a while. It was also going to cost a lot of money, certainly more than we had. Mother was forced to call the bank back in Marshall, then one of her brothers in Mineola and another in Kilgore. I remember the solemn, determined look on her face as she tried to deal with the mechanic, the garage owner, and the man who ran the cheap motel we stayed in. She was at the mercy of a bunch of strangers, all men. She was wounded, she was cornered, and she was trying not to let them see her bleed. We would get through this.

I, for my part, had adapted fairly quickly. There was a café-cantina there in Van Horn, near the motel. It had a pool table in it and I spent the entire three days shooting nine-ball with a group of Mexican boys about my age. Pool became my new interest. By the time we left town I was getting pretty good at it, and I had also picked up a few Spanish swear words.

It was Lucia, the future nun, who didn't bear up well. She sulked and pouted and stayed in the motel room the three of us were forced to share. She wouldn't even come out to eat. Mother had to take food from the café in to her. We could see her through the window in there, sitting on the bed, picking half-heartedly at her food, then returning to the little leatherbound missal with her initials on it that she always kept with her, reading in it, poring over it, and, simultaneously, telling her rosary beads. She seemed to me to be constantly on the verge of tears.

"Hey, Lucia," I said brightly the second day we were there, trying to cheer her up, "would you like to learn how to shoot some nine-ball?"

But she just looked at me, shook her head mournfully, choked back a sob, and returned to her book and her beads. She was going to make one fine nun, I decided.

When we finally got back on the road again the atmosphere in the perfidious Chevy was markedly subdued. No radio playing, no chitchat about anything we saw along the highway, not even the Burma-Shave signs we'd been accustomed to reading aloud to each other before. We seemed to be honoring Lucia's mood. The rebuilt engine sounded pretty good, but I was cautioned by mother not to go too fast, so I kept one eye on the speedometer as I drove. We still had three hundred miles to go to reach Tucson and mother was determined to finish the trip. There was never any talk of turning back.

So we eased our way through New Mexico and Arizona, stopping every so often for gas and restroom breaks at the isolated "trading posts" that served as filling stations and souvenir shops along the route, nobody saying much. This was really barren country, not at all like green and leafy East Texas. I had never seen so much *nothing*. It reminded me of the backdrops of all those Roy Rogers and Gene Autry movies I used to watch. By now we had a canvas water bag slung from the hood ornament of the car, and it was my job to stop every thirty miles or so and make sure the radiator was still full; the last thing we wanted to do was throw another rod. Las Cruces, Deming, Lordsburg, and Willcox slowly came and went, and at last, on the evening of our fifth day on the road, we limped into Tucson, which was just a sleepy desert town of 45,000 back then, not the sprawling metropolis it is today. There was an Air Force base there, and a state university, and not much else.

Sophie and her husband were glad to see us. They had a nice house in a good part of town. Sophie served us a good meal and we slept on clean, comfortable beds that night. I found a pool hall not too far from the house the next day and continued my education there. We arrived on a Tuesday and had intended to stay through the weekend. Sophie and her husband had plans to drive us out into the Sonora Desert on Saturday and show us all the interesting varieties of cactus to be found there. But by Friday mother had decided it was time for us to head back. Sophie Maranto protested, but not too vigorously. She could read mother pretty well. Lucia, however, would stay on with her sister in Tucson for the summer. I'm not sure that that was the original plan, but that was how it worked out. Maybe Lucia, with her extremely narrow comfort zone, decided she didn't want to risk another layover in Van Horn on the way back. In any event, when mother and I pulled out she wasn't with us.

We left Tucson in the early afternoon, just the two of us. And this is the part of the trip I remember best. I remember the pair of us, side by side in the front seat of that little Chevy, driving into darkness and beyond on that long-ago summer's evening. I remember the intimacy of it, and the

51

quiet pleasure: mother and son alone in their car, *their* car, plowing together through the soft, enveloping night.

Maybe the trip hadn't been such a rip-roaring success. Maybe there had been unexpected hardship and unfortunate delays. Maybe money was going to be even tighter than usual for a while now, and certain expectations—about, say, new clothes for school come fall and the like—would have to be put on hold. But we had gone through a rough patch together, mother and I, and come out on the other side of it. We hadn't let it beat us; we hadn't let it get us down. And now, with every mile that passed, we were getting closer to home: back to East Texas and its piney woods and rolling hills and muddy little rivers. Too many cactus, too much sand and too much sun weren't good for East Texans like us. We needed to get back where the grass burrs were.

"What do you think, mama?" I said at one point to the tough little woman beside me. "Will Lucia Maranto make a good nun?"

Mother was silent for a moment, thinking it over. "Well, I hope so," she said finally. "Poor thing, I can't see her making much of anything else—can you?"

I remember smiling in the darkness of the car. That seemed like a pretty good answer to me. We drove on through the night, mother and I. Outside Willcox she let me turn the radio on.

## Drugstore Days

When I was fifteen I worked for a man named Bob
Martin who owned and operated an establishment on
South Washington Avenue there in Marshall that everyone
referred to simply as "Bob Martin Drug." There must have
been a sign somewhere out front, on the plate glass window
maybe or above the door, that identified it as such, but if
there was I don't remember it. Bob Martin Drug, as the
name indicates, was a drugstore—more or less. There was
no pharmacist in residence, no medicinal herbs in back,
or anywhere else, that could be pounded and ground into
prescription cures. All we had were shelves carrying such
common, over-the-counter items as Vaseline, Bayer aspirin,
Alka-Seltzer, Sloan's Linament, Pepto-Bismol, and the like.
We also sold Kotex, Whitman's chocolates, barbecue grills,
school supplies, and contraceptives. I can still remember
the furtive look even middle-aged men would get on their
faces when they came in to ask for "Trojans" or "Sheiks."

Physically, the store wasn't much, just a long main room
with a storage area and toilet in back. The cash register sat
on a counter up front and to the right, while over on the
left, running the length of the store, were the soda fountain
and a series of padded booths, one after the other. This
part of the store was my bailiwick. I had been hired as the
soda jerk. I was Bob Martin's only employee. He and I ran
the store together. When he wasn't there, which was much
of the time, I was the man in charge. It used to get pretty
lonely in there because we never had much business.

We shared a building with a supermarket and a

53

laundromat. They never had much business either. At least that's how I remember it. Which makes me wonder now how, and why, we all kept going. The year was 1952, and maybe that's just the way it was in small towns in East Texas back then: you kept going because what else were you going to do? At Bob Martin Drug it was a good day when we took in thirty dollars. I have memories of Bob Martin coming into the store, going to the cash register, checking the meager receipts, sighing, and going back out again. That was the way he was: in and out, in and out, all day long. I never knew where he went—to the bank? home to his wife and kids? to a movie?—but when he showed up I would try to look busy. My pay as his soda jerk was only twenty cents an hour. Bob was embarrassed about this, but as he sheepishly told me, it was all he could afford. Even in 1952 twenty cents an hour wasn't much. Schoolmates of mine lucky enough to land a summer job with the highway department made the princely sum of ninety cents an hour. I would see them out on a stretch of highway holding a "Slow, Men Working" sign and think, *They're getting ninety cents an hour for that?* To compensate myself for my meager pay I regularly dipped into the cigar box holding the loose change from my soda fountain sales which I kept on a shelf behind me. I felt guilty about this at first, but eventually I got used to it. If I needed money for a weekend movie, or maybe a haircut, I would simply filch it from the cigar box when Bob wasn't around, which was usually. I think he sort of expected me to. At least that's how I rationalized it to myself.

Hot summer evenings were when we did our best soda fountain business. We closed the store at 7 p.m. each day, and about an hour before that, mindful of the approaching closing, customers would start drifting in, everybody wanting something cold to drink, or eat. I made lots of malts and milkshakes at this time, lots of ice cream sundaes and root beer floats. My right arm used to get caked with ice cream up past the elbow from reaching deep down into the big cardboard canisters to dig the ice cream out. I remember the sour smell of it after it had been on my arm for a while. Proceeds from these fountain sales would go into the cigar box for later transfer, after perhaps a small tithe to myself, to the cash register across the way.

The Korean War was in high gear in 1952 and there was much talk in the air about universal military training, or "UMT" as the newspaper headlines of the day often had it. President Truman supported the idea as did much of Congress. It would require that all U.S. males undergo mandatory military training once they reached a certain age. I forget what the age was, but one afternoon a photographer for the local paper, the *Marshall News Messenger*, showed up at Bob Martin Drug saying he wanted to take my picture for a story about the kinds of young males likely to be affected if UMT became law. He arrived unannounced, informed me of what he wanted to do, and then took a picture of me behind the soda fountain with one hand resting on one of the fountain spigots. Then he left, and the next day, sure enough, there was my picture in the paper, with a caption saying who I was, and how old, and that I was a candidate for UMT if it became law. People who came in the store said they had seen the picture and thought it was a pretty good likeness. Some wondered if it meant I was about to be drafted. I said I didn't think so, but I didn't know for sure. That's how it was in small towns back then. Very informal, very unstructured. You just sort of made life up as you went along.

I told Bob Martin about the photographer when he came in, but he didn't seem much interested. "I don't suppose he bought anything, did he?" was all he said.

Bob Martin was an interesting fellow. He was slight and sandy-haired and probably in his early thirties when I knew him. He had a wife and two small children that I hardly ever saw because he rarely brought them by the store. He spoke with a stammer that made it hard at times for him to get his words out. His face would get red and he'd be making a "chu-chu-chu" sound as he tried to get clear of his blockage. Then he would stop, compose himself, and start over again, slowly and carefully. Bob was the star of the annual Lions Loonies minstrel show, staged each spring at the City Hall Auditorium. He was "Mister Interlocutor," the master of ceremonies for the series of variety acts featuring local talent that made up the show. He interacted with the "end men" comedians, all of them in blackface as was he, told a joke or two himself, and kept things running smoothly. The show was really quite good. Marshall had a surprising amount of homegrown talent in those days: singers, dancers, jugglers, baton twirlers, and the like. All the whites in town turned out to see the Lions' Loonies. (The blacks, due to segregation, weren't allowed to.) And here's the interesting thing. Up there onstage as Mister Interlocutor, Bob Martin never stammered or stuttered. His diction was impeccable and the words flowed as freely as tap water. I always found that amazing.

When we closed Bob Martin Drug of an evening, Bob would sometimes take me with him to a café over on Grand Avenue on the east side of town for what was commonly known, in those days of rampant political incorrectness, as a "wop salad." It actually said that on the menu: "Wop Salad, a large bowl of greens, sliced tomatoes, cucumbers, and radishes, topped with slices of ham and hardboiled egg and sprinkled with parmesan or mozzarella cheese." This last was possibly what earned it the name "wop salad." Bob Martin was very fond of these salads, and I, as his charge, became fond of them too. Over our meal Bob would regale me with tales from his youth. In his twenties, it seemed, he had been a late night disc jockey for a Fort Worth radio station, and he loved telling me what that was like. He had had a partner for a while, he said. They styled themselves "Flotsam and Jetsam," after the popular hillbilly comedy duo of the time, Homer and Jethro. Bob made the spinning of records in the small hours of the morning in a deserted radio studio sound beguilingly romantic. He had a way of weaving a story that could pull you right in. Under his spell I began to see myself as a late night disc jockey at some future date, cooing into a microphone, bringing comfort to an invisible, insomniac nation. It seemed a career worth aspiring to.

Bob was witty. He could be very funny in a sardonic, been there, done that, sort of way. One evening over our wop salads he favored me with this variation on the old children's rhyme:

*Sparkle, sparkle little twink,*
*Who the hell you are, you think?*
*Way up in the sky so high,*
*Just like a damn lightbulb."*

That still makes me smile when I think about it. And that was Bob Martin. Life was no nursery rhyme as far as he was concerned. It could be a grimly earnest affair, especially if you had a wife and two kids to support and the entire take in the till at the end of the day was seven dollars and fifty cents. Might as well go have a wop salad with the help.

There was a woman named Nell Rose Worley who used to come into the store once or twice a week in the afternoons. Nell Rose had been valedictorian of her Marshall High School graduating class some years before, but now she was married to a much older man who ran a filling station on the north side of town and was rarely ever home. Like Bob Martin, she had two small children, a boy and a girl. Sometimes she had them with her, sometimes not. Nell Rose was large and heavyset. She was a great reader of novels. Her tastes ran to Lloyd C. Douglas and Mary Roberts Rhinehart. She was also a big show business buff. She had a large collection of original cast albums of Broadway musicals of the period: *Oklahoma!, South Pacific, Carousel, Guys and Dolls*, and the like. I was going through a showbiz phase myself at the time and she and I used to while away slow afternoons discussing such topics as, Who was the better all-around dancer, Gene Kelly or Fred Astaire? Was Ethel Merman likely to be cast as the lead in the movie version of "Call Me Madam" or would Hollywood opt for some glamour gal? Was Debbie Reynolds too cute to be taken seriously or was she destined to be a superstar? We could sometimes kill a whole afternoon talking about things like that.

When fall came I had to cut back on my hours at Bob Martin Drug because of school. I could only work weekends and school holidays, mostly, and as a result Bob Martin brought on board another employee for the weekdays, an older woman named Mrs. Moore, the mother of one of my high school classmates. I don't know what Bob Martin paid Mrs. Moore (that's all I ever called her) but I assume it was something more than twenty cents an hour. I got along okay with her the rare times we were in the store together, but I found her rather odd. Her husband worked downtown at a printing and stationery store, as the store manager. The Moores weren't from Marshall originally, and they had an air about them that suggested they considered themselves a little bit better than the rest of us. Mrs. Moore fancied herself a first-rate seamstress. She made all of her son Tommy's shirts and she was forever bringing her latest creation into the store for our admiration. Eventually this aroused Nell Rose's competitive instincts. She started sewing shirts for me. Over the next year or so she must have made five or six shirts for me, each of them in response to some new beauty from the sewing machine of Mrs. Moore. It became a Shirt-a-rama, with each woman trying to outsew the other. Mother, when I started bringing my new shirts home, eyed me suspiciously, but she never said anything. When I went into the Marine Corps a couple of years later, I did so wearing a shirt made for me by Nell Rose Worley. I still have in a scrapbook a picture taken on Okinawa in 1956. It shows me and a boy named John Bright flanking a cute little bar girl in the town of New Koza. The shirt I have on, a stunning gunmetal gray number with an orange plaid collar and orange plaid piping, comes straight from the House of Nell Rose.

In the fall of 1954 I went off to Paris Junior College up in Paris, Texas, to play football. When I came home on weekends I would usually check in with Bob and would occasionally help out around the store, if he needed someone. One evening we went out together for a valedictory wop salad. In early 1955, having dropped out of PJC, I enlisted in the Marines, and when I came home on my first leave after boot camp I learned to my surprise that Bob Martin Drug was no more. Bob had finally given up on store ownership as a bad bet and had taken a job with a man named Carlos Caccioppia, who held the McCulloch chainsaw franchise there in Marshall. Apparently, in the mid-50's a McCulloch chainsaw franchise amounted to a license to print money, because Carlos Caccioppia had quickly become one of the richest men in town. He had also become the town's leading Big Catholic Layman, or BCL. Mother, newly confirmed in the Catholic faith, spoke reverentially of "Mr. Caccioppia" and what he had done, and was continuing to do, for St. Joseph's Catholic Church and indeed all of St. Joseph's Parish.

I didn't run into Bob Martin on that first leave home from the Marines, although I did go by the old store and note that its building was empty now and up for lease. It must have been on my second or third leave home from the Marines, I don't remember which, that I finally ran into Bob downtown one day. He was coming out of Recknagle Drug there on the courthouse square just as I was going in. At first I didn't recognize him. His face was fuller. He had put on some weight and had lost the harried look he used to have, was beginning to appear more conventionally middle class. His clothes were nicer—a spiffy sport jacket and neatly pressed slacks—and instead of the old Nash Rambler he used to drive back when I worked for him he had a spanking new Buick Special waiting for him there at the curb. Mother had told me that "Mister Caccioppia" thought very highly of Bob and that Bob had become one of his top chainsaw salesmen.

That day outside Recknagel Drug—a real drugstore, with pharmacists and a prescription counter and everything—we didn't have long to chat. Bob was in something of a hurry for some reason (whether or not it was to go sell another chainsaw, I don't know), but we did reminisce briefly about all those wop salads we used to consume at the café on Grand Avenue, about Flotsam and Jetsam and late night radio, and the Lions' Loonies and Mister Interlocutor—which Bob informed me he'd had to give up ("It just took too much of my time")—and even about all those Whitman's samplers and barbecue grills we were never able to sell.

It was good to see Bob. I was happy for him that he seemed to be doing so well. He'd even lost his stammer. As he sped away from the curb in his new Buick Special I watched him go with a twinge of nostalgia for the good old days at Bob Martin Drug.

*Sparkle, sparkle, little twink*, I found myself thinking, a bit wistfully. *Sparkle, sparkle, little twink...*

## Saturdays at the Paramount

My wife and I don't go to the movies much anymore. The soundtracks are too loud, they run too may trailers, the morons two rows back won't shut up: all the usual geezer complaints. These days when we get the itch we mostly let the movies come to us, via DVD or Turner Classic Movies, and we enjoy them (or, often as not, fail to) in the privacy of our own living room.

It wasn't always this way, though. In my long-ago youth I was an avid moviegoer. In fact, when it came to entertainment, moviegoing was mainly what we did back then. I was cinemate long before I was literate.

There were two theaters in my hometown of Marshall, Texas, the stinky old rundown Lynn and the tonier, more up-ticket Paramount, both of them on Washington Avenue just north of the courthouse square. The Lynn offered westerns and serials and other grade-B fare, and was where you went as a little kid, plunking down your nine cents for the Saturday afternoon double feature, plus cartoons, plus the umpteenth installment of *Don Winslow of the Coast Guard.* The Paramount was where you graduated to at about age thirteen. It showed all the major-studio first-run films on a schedule that, as I remember it, had them rotating in and out of town at the rate of about three each week, the Saturday-Sunday feature being the big one. In high school, the Paramount was where we took our dates.

How many hours must I have spent in the cloistered darkness of the Paramount Theater? A thousand? Two thousand? Three thousand? It seems to me now, looking back on it, that I was there, inside, intent, popcorn and juju-bees in hand, every time the feature changed. So if you figure three times a week for, say, eight years, that comes to, my God, 1,200 movies! And if you figure two and a half hours per movie, counting the cartoon, newsreel and "previews," as we called them back then, that comes to, yes, 3,000 hours.

And that doesn't even count the midnight shows on Saturday or the foreign-film series sponsored by the Altrusa (women's) Club one night a month on Tuesdays.

In high school, those midnight shows were a cultural must. Everybody in our crowd attended. You went to see and be seen, usually after you'd taken your date for the evening home. I remember one midnight show in particular. It was called *The Thing* and it scared the bejesus out of us. Set up in the Arctic at an isolated military outpost, it was a well-crafted space-alien thriller (directed by the legendary Howard Hawks, as I would later learn) that managed to push all the right terror buttons at all the right times. By movie's end it had managed to reduce us in the audience to a quivering, submissive heap. There were hulking high school football players who refused to drive home alone, pretty teenaged homecoming queens sobbing softly on the sofas in the lobby. James Arness of *Gunsmoke* fame, suitably got up in creepy space-alien attire, played "The Thing." It was his first movie role. He was, in the film, the consummate Bad Guy. That he would eventually become TV's Marshal Dillon, that medium's consummate Good Guy, says something about the arc even a successful actor's career can travel.

The Paramount's foreign-film series offered up culture of a different order. For a town of its size (about 18,000 souls) Marshall had always taken its culture seriously. I can remember hearing a performance of the Dallas Symphony Orchestra, with Antal Dorati conducting, in Marshall's City Hall Auditorium when I was about ten. Of the foreign films brought to us by the Altrusa Club ladies, I recall seeing and enjoying *The Red Shoes* with Moira Shearer and Marius Goring, Alexander Korda's *The Thief of Baghdad*, Vittorio de Sica's *The Bicycle Thief*, and Roberto Rossellini's *Open City*. I also remember ogling the fetching Silvana Mangano in her soaked peasant's blouse in *Bitter Rice*, which somehow slipped past the local censors.

But it was the regular fare, the three-times-weekly Hollywood offerings, that shaped our lives. Like the one before it, ours was a moviegoing generation. My mother's generation, in the 1920's-30's, was the first fully cinematic one. Ours, in the 1940's-50's, was the second, and last, one. After that, television began to leach away the magic. When, during the millennial observances of the year 2000, lists were gotten up of the past century's 100 "best" this and 100 "best" that, I found to my mild chagrin that I, a former teacher of literature and writing, had read slightly fewer than half of the mentioned novels. But I had seen all but two (*Raging Bull* and *Dances with Wolves*) of the top 100 movies. That's called influence.

The movies taught my generation (and mother's) how to be in this world, what our place was and what, whether we liked it or not, to think about it. It used to bother me to no end as a kid, for example, to see the constant Hollywood stereotype of "the Texan" thrown up on the screen in front of me. He was always tall and lanky, and he wore cowboy boots and a big hat, spoke with an atrocious drawl, and if the setting was contemporary was usually a rich "awlman." By the time I was in high school I considered myself pretty cool, and that stereotype, it seemed to me, had nothing at all to do with me, who was anything but rich and had never even owned a pair of cowboy boots. It was a time of stereotypes, of course, and the two favorite targets, for some reason, seemed to be Texas and Brooklyn, New York. In every war movie of the period there had to be a mildly outrageous character from each place who took turns serving as the

63

butt for everyone else's humor. It was a kind of shorthand for the democratic melting pot, I see now, but back then I didn't get it, and it really used to rankle. Don't call me "Tex."

But beyond the stereotypes, the movies taught us, as various cultural historians have pointed out, how to conduct ourselves in our everyday lives. I learned it was possible to walk gracefully and still be manly, for instance, by watching John Wayne stride across the screen in such films as The Searchers and Red River. I learned how to match pants with jacket and socks with both by observing Gene Kelly and Gower Champion in movies like *An American in Paris* and *Lovely To Look At*. And I learned how to hold and smoke a cigarette by watching Humphrey Bogart in *Casablanca* and *To Have and Have Not*. I even received a graduate course in cigarette-smoking from an actor named Sterling Hayden. I no longer remember the name of the movie, but I can still see Hayden, having been offered by a lady friend one of those new-fangled filtertip cigarettes, contemptuously snapping off the offending filter before lighting up. Yes! Of course! That was how it was to be done. None of those mitigating little mini-cylinders for us men, thank you. We wanted our carcinogens straight and undiluted.

And speaking of socks—as I just was, briefly—I can remember reading in one of the movie magazines of the day (*Modern Screen*, maybe, or *Photoplay*) that Tony Curtis, who had been born poor and Jewish and named Bernie Schwartz in the Bronx, boasted that as a rising Hollywood star he never wore the same pair of socks twice. He began each day, he said, with a brand-new pair. For a long time that became the definition of making it for me: a new pair of socks, fresh from the men's store, every day of the week.

Tony Curtis. Rock Hudson. Tab Hunter. For a while there these were the top three up-and-coming leading men. I remember Rock's first movie, *Fighter Squadron*. In it, he had one line: "You'd better get yourself another blackboard." And I remember reading that it took about three dozen takes for him to get the line right. But after that it was clear sailing for what all of us agreed was the best-looking man of our generation. We had no idea that Rock, and Tab too, were gay, of course. And if you had told us, we wouldn't have believed you. Tab had played Danny Forrester in the movie *Battle Cry* which had been instrumental in my decision, at age eighteen, to join the Marines. Tab Hunter gay? Get outta here. Tell that to the Marines.

I had a friend named Mickey Mauldin in high school, and he and I went through a phase during which we were convinced we were the smartest two people in town. We used to try to demonstrate this on Saturday afternoons in the Paramount by commenting, often loudly, on what we saw going on up on the screen. We were particularly good at spotting anachronisms. Pneumatic tire tracks in the sand of a Western, for instance. Or Roman soldiers wearing wristwatches. Mickey once spotted a powerline snaking its way across the horizon in a movie about Robin Hood of Sherwood Forest. If the film failed to come up to our (fairly high) standard of adequate cinema entertainment we would amuse ourselves—and the others around us, we confidently assumed—by engaging in a sort of running patter about its shortcomings—much like the louts of today who have succeeded in driving my wife and I from the local Cineplex. Only, we were witty, Mickey and I. And lots of fun to listen to. Honest!

The late 40's and early 50's were the golden age of the Hollywood musical. Why this should have been so, I'm not sure. Maybe it had something to do with the perfection of the Technicolor process, or the new wide-angle camera lenses then being introduced. I don't know. But beginning in about 1948 we were treated at the Paramount—as others were being treated elsewhere around the nation, of course—to a steady stream of musicals. Many of them were so-called "biopics": pictorial biographies of famous singers and songwriters: Al Jolson, George M. Cohan, Irving Berlin,

Jerome Kern, Harry Ruby and Bert Kahn, etc. My favorite of these movies, not a biopic, was one that spoofed the early days of Hollywood film-making. It was called *Singin' in the Rain*. It came out in 1952 and seemed to represent a coming together and culmination of all that was best in the genre. It starred Gene Kelly, Donald O'Connor and Debbie Reynolds, singing and dancing to some of the best popular music from the 1920's. I was captivated by it, and saw it half a dozen times. And I was pleased to see decades later that it ranked in the top ten on that millennial list of the all-time best movies, confirming to me that my taste as a kid hadn't been all that bad.

*Singin' in the Rain* was by far Debbie Reynolds' best movie. Everything else she did was easily forgettable. Cute little Debbie. Born in El Paso but grew up in LA.

Elizabeth Taylor stole her man away, in one of the shoddier movie-colony escapades of the day. Her "man" was the singer Eddie Fisher, and I still remember a tabloid photograph of her in toreador pants and sandals, the couple's little daughter (the future Carrie Fisher of *Star Wars*) in hand, publicly upbraiding the clueless, cast-down Fisher for his flagrant, much-publicized infidelities with Taylor. If ever an expression earned the adjective "hangdog," Fisher's, in that photo, was it.

Is it just me, or did the actresses back then seem to have more stature, more oomph than those seeking to beguile us today? Elizabeth Taylor, of course: she of the violet eyes and Devon-in-the-mist complexion; every teenaged boy's ideal of the perfect woman in those days. (Has anyone ever looked prettier than she did in *Elephant Walk* and *A Place in the Sun*?) But others too. My favorite for a time was Virginia Mayo, the slightly cross-eyed but dropdead-beautiful blonde who co-starred with everybody from Danny Kaye to Ronald Reagan in such films as *The Secret Life of Walter Mitty* and *She's Working Her Way Through College*. Mayo, unlike Taylor, could also sing and dance, though not particularly well. I could look at her up there on the screen for hours, though, and never grow tired.

Mother's favorites tended toward the austere, the regal. Irene Dunne and Greer Garson and Joan Crawford, though she did kind of like the feisty, no-necked little Claudette Colbert, especially with Clark Gable in *It Happened One Night*. I think mother, never a very sunny woman, sort of saw herself as an Irene Dunne figure who'd had the bad luck to be trapped in low-rent East Texas.

The movies began to change for the worse, it seems to me, in the sixties. Faced with the growing challenge from TV they chose the easy route of graphic violence, explicit sex and naughty language to try to lure their audience back. Most people from my generation would agree, I think, that the violence in particular quickly became off-putting. In our day villains expired quietly, decorously, after having been dispatched by James Cagney or Humphrey Bogart with a single, well-placed (blank) shot. Nowadays, audiences have to endure gore and mayhem of the duration and magnitude of the Battle of Antietam, and oftentimes endure it close up and in slow motion. This current and continuing emphasis on gore can be traced, it seems to me, to a single scene in a single movie from 1967: Arthur Penn's *Bonnie and Clyde*. The scene, of course, is the climactic ambush of Bonnie and Clyde by federal agents at movie's end. When the feds open up with their fusillade of automatic-weapons fire, some thin streak of directorial genius in Penn inspired him to suddenly slow the film speed down and allow us—force us—to watch the slaughter for many long seconds in exquisite slow motion. It became a ballet of death, a veritable dance of destruction, as bullet after bullet after death-dealing bullet (seemingly) punctured the suddenly vulnerable hides of Faye Dunaway as "Bonnie" and Warren Beatty as "Clyde." The movie was a huge box-office success and eventual multi-Oscar winner; critics like Pauline Kael of *The New Yorker* rushed to praise the graphic depiction of slaughter at the end, and moviegoers have been putting up with—or feasting on, depending on your taste—similar, often even more blood-splatteringly graphic, scenes ever since.

I went home to Marshall recently on a visit. The Paramount Theater building is still there on Washington Avenue, though much of the town has now moved out nearer the new interstate highway, leaving the former downtown "business district" something of a shell of its former self. The Paramount building is still there, along with its "Paramount" marquee, but the theater itself is long gone. What remains in its place is a consignment center, occupying that once hallowed ground. A sad, sad turn of events for someone with as many memories of those long-ago afternoons and evenings as I have. Where the flickering image of Tony Curtis, he of the brand new socks, once presided, now only tables piled with secondhand clothing are to be found.

The architecture—maybe that's too fancy a word; the layout, rather—of the old Paramount, my old Paramount, was, if not unique, then at least out of the ordinary. There was a typical marquee out front, with the traditional multi-bulbed lighting arrangement spelling out the theater's name above the big black-and-white letterboard announcing the current feature. The ticket box sat just in under the marquee and was flanked on either side by double doors, one set for entering, the other for leaving. But then, beyond there, things got different, because past those double doors stretched a longish interior corridor leading down to yet another set of double doors, and it was only past there that you entered (or exited) the theater lobby, with its snackbar and darkened, curtained-off proximity to the inner sanctum, where the magic took place. The corridor was tiled and slightly downwardly inclined, as I recall it, and was lined on either side with glassed-in playbills promoting coming attractions for weeks in advance. All of this gave a certain hall-of-mirrors feeling to things and added to the anticipatory excitement, particularly on those sell-out evenings when the incoming crowd had to stand out there in the corridor and wait, impatience mounting by the minute, for the theater to empty before entering.

"How was it?" you'd ask the exiting moviegoers.

And, "Great!" they might say, or, "You're not gonna believe the ending!"

And the excitement, already palpable, would ratchet up a notch.

I have been in movie houses all over the world in my more than seven decades of moviegoing, and I can honestly say that none of them ever surpassed the Paramount Theater on Washington Avenue when it came to ambience and proper attention to the necessities of the communal ritual that small-town movie watching used to be. And I attribute a lot of it to that tiled and glassed corridor, that anteroom to wonder, in which I spent so many eager, antsy moments as a youth. Certainly, today's little cineplex boxes, with their shrunken screens and packing-crate dimensions, can't hold a candle—make that an usher's flashlight—to it. One more reason why, these days, my wife and I stay home.

# Pin Boys

I think of it as our bowling summer. We were around thirteen at the time, which would make it the summer between the eighth and ninth grades, I guess. Bowling seized our fancy for that brief period and we gave ourselves over to it, day after day, all through the hot months of June, July and August. Then when September came, with school and everything that brought with it, our interest, like a summer shower, quickly went away.

There were four of us usually, and we discovered the bowling alley during one of our daily bike rides to the city swimming pool. The pool was at one end of City Park and the bowling alley, housed in the last of a series of nondescript industrial buildings across from the softball field, was at the other. It had been there all along, apparently; we'd just never noticed it before. There was a sign out front that said "Marshall Bowlanes," but it wasn't very big and you could miss it if you weren't looking for it.

Inside, the bowling alley was cramped and sort of dingy. There were only six lanes. The counter where you rented shoes and paid for your games was up front on the left as you came in. Games cost fifteen cents a line and rental shoes, as I remember it, were a dime.

A Mr. and Mrs. Ford ran the place. They were about our parents' age and seemed like a nice enough couple, although Mrs. Ford didn't put up with any nonsense. No running indoors was one of her rules, and no horseplay. No spitting in the big, sand-filled ashtrays was another. ("You wouldn't do that at home, would you?")

Mark Jackman was the first of our group to break a hundred. He and his family had only recently moved to town from Dallas, though, and he had bowled before. For the rest of us during that first week, gutter balls were the norm. This game wasn't as easy as it looked.

Gradually we got the hang of it, however, and before long we were all routinely breaking a hundred. Then two hundred became the goal. I still remember the first time I broke two hundred. Mrs. Ford announced it over the microphone she kept by the cash register. Then she called me over to the counter and awarded me my prize: a little red tin ashtray with the words "I'm a Member of the Two-Hundred Club" printed around the edges. I took it home and showed it to mother, who wasn't greatly impressed.

After a couple of weeks we felt right at home at the bowling alley. Soon we were exploring the place between games. The year was 1949 and pins at the Marshall Bowlanes, unlike those at some of the more up-to-date facilities elsewhere, were still being set by hand. We had observed the little black boys about our age hopping down into the pits to rerack our knocked-over pins and put our bowling balls up into the chutes that returned them to us, had noticed their wide white eyes following us from the semi-concealment of their perches above the racks. And gradually we began to drift down to the doorway separating the front of the bowling alley from the back and, in ones and twos, to make our way through it.

It was another world back there. Primitive, musty, dark. Nothing had been painted or improved, and all the raw, exposed lumber gave the place the look and feel of something unfinished, or not meant to be finished, like scaffolding, or the bowels of some old sailing ship. Our eyes took a while to adjust to the lack of light. The smell near the pin-setting stalls was high, a combination of sweat and dirt and uncleanliness, plus a certain sour-sweetness that was not unpleasant. Slowly we made out the faces that had turned in the stalls to take us in.

"Whatchall want?" a voice said.

"Nothin'. We're just lookin' around."

"Ain't nothin' back here."

"We just wanta see."

"Ain't nothin' to see."

But before many more days had passed we were over into the pits with these dark boys, asking to be shown how to set pins. And as the days went by we began to spend as much time in the back with the pin boys as we did up front, bowling. There was nothing much to pin-setting, really. Just a matter of gathering up the knocked-down ones and loading them into the overhead rack, then retrieving the ball and placing it in the return chute. Of course, the balls and the pins were fairly heavy, so there was an amount of effort involved, and to pull down the fully loaded rack to reset all ten pins for the next bowler required some serious grunting and bracing of feet and swinging from the lever bar, but on the whole it was more fun than it was work. At least in the beginning. At least for us.

It was when we discovered that the pin boys were being paid a nickel for each line of pins they set that things began to change. A nickel a line meant twenty cents if there were four bowlers to the game. And five games with four bowlers each meant a dollar, which for a thirteen-year-old, in those days, was real money.

*Why them?* it soon occurred to us. *Why not us?*

We went to Mrs. Ford and asked to be allowed to set pins.

Sure, she said. She didn't see any reason why not. There were several afternoon leagues of bowlers, housewives and second-shift workers at the brick factory and the like, which usually kept the place busy right up until supper time, and she and Mr. Ford could probably use a few extra hands in back.

"Talk to the little nigras," she said. "Work it out amongst yourselves. And no horseplay, you hear me?"

We began by spelling the black pin boys from time to

time during league play. When all six lanes were active it could get pretty hectic in back, and after setting pins for five or six games in a row even the sturdiest among them needed a breather. That's when Mark Jackman or Tommy Murphy or Jerry Barrett or I would jump in, our shirts off, grinning wildly, determined to show the customers up front how pin-setting really ought to be done.

Boy, did we gather up those pins! Boy, did we slam down those racks with a satisfying clatter! Boy, did we fire those bowling balls back!

I think I made about three dollars my first week of setting pins. Not a bad haul. It was twice my allowance, and enough to pay for all my own bowling, plus a daily Dr. Pepper or two, and still have some left over for a Saturday movie.

The money was so good, in fact, and the work so comparatively simple, that other kids in our neighborhood began to take an interest, even a couple of the older ones. By mid-summer as many as eight or nine of us were showing up at the bowling alley each day ready to bowl and set pins.

The black pin boys didn't know how to deal with this. They didn't know who to turn to. There was a railroad track running behind the bowling alley and the other industrial buildings, with several empty boxcars parked on it. The black pin boys had their headquarters in one of these boxcars. It was where they retreated to during slack periods to smoke their cigarettes and do whatever else black kids did when they were loafing. And as gradually we began to muscle them out of their jobs we could see them out there watching us and muttering among themselves.

By late July we had just about driven them out entirely. There were enough of us white kids showing up each day to handle even the busiest periods of league play. Mr. and Mrs. Ford didn't interfere. They were happy as long as the pins got set.

So we bowled a while and set pins a while, bowled a while and set pins a while, and in that fashion the long hot days of summer slipped away. Occasionally we might hear a racket from out back: small rocks bouncing off the rear wall of the building, muffled shouts of "Ofay!"—things like that—but nothing to be concerned about.

Then one day in early August we arrived at the bowling alley to find there had been a fire. Someone had apparently taken a match to some old rags and newspapers in one of the boxcars out back. It wasn't much of a fire, the fire department didn't even have to be called, but it did char the inside of the boxcar pretty badly, and it left an acrid, smoky smell hanging in the air for several days. Nobody knew exactly how the fire had started, or who started it, but since the boxcar that burned was the one the black pin boys used for their headquarters we had our suspicions.

"Idden that just like a bunch of n-----rs?" someone said. "Set fahr to their own place."

After that we didn't see the black pin boys anymore. They quit coming around. Maybe they were afraid of being blamed for the fire. I don't know. But for whatever reason, the boxcars out back, including the burnt one, sat empty and silent. When we looked out there, nothing stirred.

By late August, though, we had other things on our minds. Fall football practice would be getting underway soon and it was time to start running our laps over at the school track, doing our push-ups and sit-ups, "getting in shape," as it was called. Slowly, one by one, we began to phase out our appearances at the bowling alley. By the last weekend in August we had stopped showing up entirely. On one of those final afternoons Mrs. Ford said to me, "Looks like you all have lost your interest, doesn't it? I'm running short of pin setters."

"Yes'm," I said. "Sorry to leave you in a bind like this, but it's football."

Football was big in East Texas. It took precedence. Everyone understood that.

"Well, don't worry about it," Mrs. Ford said. "Go

practice your ball. I'll send Mr. Ford over to the colored section in the pickup. He'll come back with a whole truckload of pin boys."

And that's what she did.

Were they the ones we'd displaced? Probably not, but who knew? Or cared?

As for us, though, we rarely ever bowled again after that. And I never came close to breaking two hundred again. When the next summer rolled around we spent it, day after sun-splashed day, out on Caddo Lake just east of Marshall, being pulled behind Tommy Murphy's older brother's sixty-horse Evinrude.

I think of that as our water-skiing summer.

Father and son, circa 1940

Mother as a young woman, on a street somewhere, packages and purse in hand

Mother and I posing in costume for a street photographer in
Nuevo Laredo, circa 1945

The author in full Huck Finn mode, age ten or eleven

The Circle D Square Dance Club gathered for an outing to Caddo Lake, with "Neil Pomeroy" and I side by side in the back row, right

Gathered around the piano at the Resch's house. That's me in the foreground, with Kathleen Resch beside me and Father Claybaugh at the keys.

This football action shot appeared in the Marshall High School yearbook for 1954, with a caption reading simply, "Uh! Oof! Ouch!" That's me, upended, with the ball and "Neil Pomeroy," number 64, in the background.

My cousin Roger Hughes (left) and I, looking a lot like brothers, at a family reunion in the 1980s, the overturned icebox no longer our joint shame

The indomitable Kathleen Resch holding up a large crab for our inspection—just where, I'm not sure

This picture was taken on Okinawa in 1956. That's me on the left, trying to look tough, which of course I wasn't, being by nature an overly sensitive mama's boy.

Also taken on Okinawa, with me on the left sporting one of the shirts Nell Rose Worley made for me. The boy on the right is my friend, John Bright. The name of the cute little bar girl in the middle is, unfortunaely, lost to history.

Mother in her lab coat at DXL, with an unidentified colleague

Mother and I on the porch of our house in Slippery Rock, PA, when I was teaching at the college there in the '70s, with my children (left to right) John, Ruth, and Peter

Mother at her retirement party at ICI, wearing an attractive outfit
I had never seen her in before

Sally Belle Hughes Lacy (December 6, 1914 - December 31, 1986

# When Country Was Country

Floyd Tillman died not too long ago at the age of eighty-eight. And the year before him, at the remarkable age of a hundred and one, so did Jimmie Davis. Two titans of country music, gone now to that great Louisiana Hayride in the sky. And with them, two frail reminders—quite possibly the last—of the way country music used to be.

In the smalltown East Texas of my boyhood these two men were a tremendous presence. They were bigger than Crosby, bigger than Sinatra. They put Glenn Miller in the shade. One of my first memories has to do with Jimmie Davis's "You Are My Sunshine." I must have been three or four years old at the time and had recently got badly tangled up with some barbed wire while trying to crawl through a fence. The Davis song was constantly on the radio in those days, and when whoever the singer of the moment was came to the part that goes, *When I awoke dear I was mistaken/ and I hung my head and cried,* I would instantly flash on a little boy (me) with his head hung up in barbed wire. I carried that image around with me for years, triggered every time I heard the Davis song, which must have numbered eventually in the hundreds.

(Similarly, when I heard in those days the Ernest Tubb song "Walkin' the Floor Over You," having at my command at the time only one definition of the word "over," I always used to get a mental picture of someone stomping around upstairs, on the floor above me.)

My father died when I was five. He was a long haul trucker and was killed when his rig, loaded down with roofing materials, slid off a rain-slick highway near Woodville, down near Houston, and hit a tree. Driving a truck had been his day job. In his youth, before moving to Texas and meeting the girl who would become my mother, he had had his own country band, "Les Lacy and His Alabama Ramblers," and he still picked and sang for the neighbors, and whoever else would listen, in the series of little sawmill towns where we lived in those Depression-haunted times.

Because I was so young when he died, I have few memories of my father. What memories I retain center mostly on his music. Three songs in particular I associate with him. I think of them as "his" songs. They were the ones, it seems to me in memory, that showcased him at his best, the ones he most often liked to play and sing. First and foremost of these was Floyd Tillman's "It Makes No Difference Now." For years, well into high school and beyond, the surest way for me to resurrect my father's memory was to begin to sing to myself, either aloud or under my breath, depending on where I was, the lyrics to this Tillman classic:

*Makes no difference now what kind of life fate hands me,*
*I'll get along without you now it's plain to see,*
*After all is said and done I'll still get by somehow.*
*I don't worry 'cause it makes no difference now...*

It's a song about the stoic acceptance of the way things are, and although the second verse (*It was just a year ago when I first met you, dear*) makes it clear that what's being sung about is a broken love affair, the words when coupled with the music would seem to support a broader application: that of a son determined to get used to the fact of a departed father, say, or even of a whole class of people striving to keep their chins up and keep on going despite the poverty of their circumstances.

The other two songs evoke similar feelings from me.

They are "Be Honest with Me," the old Gene Autry and Fred Rose favorite, and Jimmie Davis's "Nobody's Darling But Mine." Like the Tillman song, each of these is simple, straightforward, and to the point. Each addresses the listener directly, with no frills and no digressions. All three seem to have been crafted expressly for a lone male singer and a lone acoustic guitar. You can hear the pain in them, certainly, but you can also hear the dignity, the sense of distance, a certain becoming reserve. I may be suffering, they say, but I don't intend to wear it on my sleeve. *Be honest, be faithful, be kind,* implores the Davis song, and the Autry song, *If you really love me, be honest with me.* Also, *Come lay your sweet head on my brow,* says the Davis song, a gorgeous line that has always seemed to me the very essence of folk poetry.

"Lay your sweet head on my brow." Who even thinks that way anymore? Who has the serenity of soul for it?

This was the music of a particular people at a particular time. The time was the Depression-era thirties and the early-wartime forties and the people were a largely rural, white, Southern underclass. They were aware of who they were, and although it would be too much to say they were proud of it, they weren't, by God, ashamed of it either. At least they pretended not to be. They were the bottom dogs, right down there next to the Negroes (whom they naturally despised). They couldn't tell you with any certainty who was running the show, they just knew it wasn't them. They drove the trucks, worked in the sawmills and turpentine plants, raised hell on weekends, and hoped there would still be a job there waiting when they showed up, reasonably sober, on Monday. Hollywood and Tin Pan Alley could sing of "Dancing Cheek to Cheek" and "Flying Down To Rio," but they knew a different reality. Adultery, drunkenness, treachery, divorce, all those pathologies of the poor: this was the terrain of their daily lives. They enlisted in the Army to better themselves! And wound up in places like North Africa and Sicily and Okinawa, dodging German and Japanese industrialists' bullets and returning fire with American industrialists' bullets of their own. Somebody was getting rich somewhere, they knew, but—again—it wasn't them. When you're down at the bottom looking up, life can get confusing. Everything begins to seem like a trick. Maybe that's why their music cried out for honesty, faithfulness, and the like. They hadn't had a lot of that so far and thought they'd like to try some. And if it didn't work out in the end, as so often it did not—well, hell, old hoss, what did you expect?

*I don't worry 'cause it makes no difference now.*

It was music to live by. Music to strap on and wear, like armor. It posited a world of hardship and saw disappointment as part of the natural order of things. It was also laconic in the extreme, as befitted a people not used to being listened to at length. The lyrics to a typical Cole Porter song—"You're the Top," "Begin the Beguine," "Let's Do It"—might run on for pages, as might those of other longwinded Tin Pan Alley types such as Irving Berlin and Harold Arlen. But the lyrics and the musical notations *combined* to the Tillman, Davis and Autry songs mentioned above could be easily transcribed onto the back of a paper napkin. About a hundred words apiece is what their authors could spare for them. They employ few chord changes. There are no bridges, no refrains, just two or three brief verses and that's it. The audience for whom such music was intended probably wouldn't have sat still for much more. They didn't have the time, didn't have the leisure to. Those long songs with fancy lyrics (*You'll find that you're in the rotogravure*—what the hell was a "rotogravure"?) were for another echelon of humanity somewhere else. Just give it to us straight and simple, this audience said. Just spit it out in our hand.

Then one day in 1940 when he didn't have much of anything else to do, a flamboyant country bandleader named Bob Wills jotted down some lyrics to a little tune he'd written years earlier and decided to call the result "San Antonio Rose." And suddenly the world of country music got a whole lot bigger. "I went from eatin' hamburgers to eatin' steaks," Wills told one interviewer. "San Antonio Rose" became, by all accounts, the single most popular song among GIs in World War II, no matter what part of the country they hailed from, North or South, East or West. And when the war ended country music radio stations began popping up in places like Cincinnati and Chicago and Detroit. Before long they were all over the country—even in New York City! even in Boston!—and almost overnight, it seemed, the rural, smalltown South had lost it's exclusive franchise on something it had been accustomed to calling its own.

I can remember being in junior high school in the late forties when a song by a relative newcomer named Hank Williams began to dominate the nation's airwaves. The song was "Lovesick Blues," and although it was early enough in country music's transition from a regional to a national phenomenon that we in East Texas could take a measure of pride in the fact that a good ol' boy from nearby Louisiana was knocking the best Tin Pan Alley had to offer right off the charts, still, the song itself, if we paused in our preening long enough to actually listen to what it was saying, wasn't anything to brag about. Was, in fact, pretty embarrassing:

*I got a feelin' called the blue-oo-oo-s, oh Lawd*
*Since my baby said goodbye.*
*And I don't know what I'm doin',*
*All I do is sit and sigh-eye-eye, oh Lawd*
*That last long day she said goodbye,*
*Well, Lawd, I thought I would cry.*
*She'll do me, she'll do you, she's got that kind of lovin'*
*Lawd, I love to hear her when she calls me*
*Sweet da-a-a-a-dy, such a beautiful dream*
*I hate to think it all over,*

*I've lost my heart it seems.*
*I've grown so used to you somehow,*
*Well, I'm nobody's sugar daddy now*
*And I'm lo-o-onesome*
*I've got the lovesick blues.*

The lyrics weren't gibberish, exactly, but they came close. And as country music went, they were a far cry from the simple dignity of "It Makes No Difference Now" and "Be Honest With Me." "San Antonio Rose," for all its crowd-pleasing tunefulness, had at least some elements of the old country soul in it, and its lyrics contained a hint of poetry here and there (*Lips so sweet and tender, like petals falling apart/ speak once again of my Rose, my own*). This Williams song, "Lovesick Blues," had none of that. It was all flash and gimmickry and verbal gymnastics. It was prolix. It wallowed in its own silliness. It seemed proud—*proud!*—of it's lack of sincerity.

Williams would go on to write and record any number of "crossover" hits after that, everything from the further silliness of "Jambalaya" and "Kaw-Liga" to the stock tearjerkery of "Cold, Cold Heart," but something irretrievable was beginning to go out of country music. At least out of country music as I had first heard it as a little boy—all those simple, heartfelt melodies of love and loss and making do.

Ironically, Tillman himself would write and record a song in the late forties that helped accelerate the shift to this new breed of music. The song was "Slippin' Around," and it enjoyed tremendous success month after month at the dawning of the fifties, topping the charts in both "hillbilly" and "pop" categories when it was covered as a duet by Margaret Whiting and Jimmy Wakeley . It was a song that generated an amount of controversy at first because of the subject matter of its lyrics: adultery. Never had American pop music addressed such an issue so overtly. Adultery?

That was something the lower orders engaged in, wasn't it? That was something *those* people did. Yes, Cole Porter, in his clever way, might slyly suggest that "Anything Goes." He might even urge "Let's Do It." But he was just referring to a "glimpse of stocking," wasn't he? And just urging us to "fall in love," wasn't he? Wasn't he?

> *Seems we always have to slip around*
> *To be together, dear*
> *Slippin' around*
> *Afraid we might be found.*
>
> *I know I can't forget you*
> *And I've got to have you near*
> *But we just have to slip around*
> *And live in constant fear.*

went the lyrics to Tillman's song, and an America being force fed "Father Knows Best" and "Kukla, Fran and Ollie" on that newfangled audience-agglomerator, television, didn't quite know what to make of them. But America learned, and adjusted, soon enough. "Slippin' Around" shot all the way up to Number One on the "Lucky Strike Hit Parade," and before long even the squeaky-clean likes of Snooky Lanson and Rosemary Clooney were singing it.

The Whiting-Wakeley rendition remained the standard, though. That was the one that sold all the records. And in its way it might almost serve as a metaphor for what was happening to country music. Margaret Whiting, after all, was a well-known, well-established pop singer, a graduate of the big band era of American pop and swing. Her previous hits had been such standard Tin Pan Alley effusions as "A Tree in the Meadow" and "Come Rain or Come Shine." Her mainstream pedigree, in other words, was near perfect. Jimmy Wakeley, on the other hand, was just a third-string singing cowboy, a near nonentity well back of Roy Rogers and Gene Autry when it came to name recognition and public acclaim. It was clear that he was to be seen as the junior partner in the pairing. Whiting was the "name." Uptown was condescending to Mayberry RFD, allowing it into the parlor. The movers and shakers of the U.S. recording industry were bringing country music indoors, knocking the bark off, taming it for the Donna Reed-adoring masses.

After that the distinction began to blur. Hank Williams was country but also pop, as the continuing nationwide success of songs such as "Cold, Cold Heart" would attest. Patsy Cline was country too but "Crazy," written by Willie Nelson, was a runaway pop chart hit from sea to shining sea. Then came Dolly Parton, she of the spectacular chest and the less-than-spectacular voice who would very quickly begin to eschew the Grand Ol' Opry in favor of near-weekly appearances on Johnny Carson's "Tonight Show." Show biz. Glitter and glitz. ("Isn't she cute? Listen to how she talks!") And after that it was just a hop, skip and a jump to Garth Brooks and the Dixie Chicks and the final ascendance of country music.

The music of the underclass had finally arrived, but in the process it had also disappeared, having been swallowed up by the great autonomic mulching machine that is American consumer culture. This country has a genius for that, of course. It can co-opt a counter trend quicker than you can say Whole Earth Catalog, or Volkswagen beetle, or granola bar. We still have a white Southern underclass—all those Wal-Mart shoppers, all those NASCAR enthusiasts, all those Kentucky Fried Chicken "extra crispy" diners—but it has lost its identity by now and is not much different, really, from its counterpart white *Northern* underclass, or for that matter from the newly arrived Hispanic underclass or the old, established black one. Everyone buys their clothes at Target these days, their burgers at McDonald's, their CDs at Best Buy, their DVDs at Red Box. Everyone, North and South, black, brown and white, sounds pretty much the same.

My father, the truckdriving country singer manque, belonged to that class of white Southern yeomanry for whom dressing up, back there in the thirties and forties, meant putting on a pair of clean, starched khakis and a white "dress" shirt with the cuffs turned back. Except for the ones he was buried in, he never owned a suit and tie. The khakis and the white shirt and the thin-soled brown shoes he wore on dress-up occasions were like a uniform, and a badge. Just as the Lucky Strike cigarettes he smoked were (Lucky Strikes and Camels being the "manly" brands back then), and the long-necked bottles of Pearl beer he drank. All these things said, This is who I am. This is what I represent. And if you don't like it, what are you going to do about it? Fred Astaire in his top hat and tails, with his monogrammed lighters and his champagne evenings with Ginger Rogers on his arm, occupied an entirely different universe. My father—who would strike a kitchen match with his thumbnail to light his Luckies—could not have communicated with that crowd even if he had wanted to. The gulf between them was just too wide. They were different species. Separate and distinct.

Similarly, the music each promulgated and preferred had little if anything in common.

*Heaven, I'm in heaven,* (sang Fred)
*And my heart beats so that I can hardly speak*
*And I seem to find the happiness I seek*
*When we're out together dancing cheek to cheek*

Whereas my father, after he had pulled up a straight chair in our little kerosene-lit front room out there on the highway somewhere between Lufkin and Nacogdoches, after he had seated himself and adjusted his tuning pegs, strummed his frets a time or two experimentally and taken one last swig from his bottle of Pearl, would answer for his—for *our*—side (without, of course, knowing he was doing so):

> *It was just a year ago when I first met you, dear*
> *I learned to love you and I thought you loved me too,*
> *But that's all over now and I'll get by somehow,*
> *I don't worry 'cause it makes no difference now.*

# Up in the Ozarks

We were on our way to Kansas City to visit some of Neil's relatives. He and I had been doing the driving while his mother and his little sister, Carol Kay, relaxed in back. We were in the Pomeroy's new black Dodge, but Mr. Pomeroy, Neil's father, wasn't with us. He was manager of the phone company back home and couldn't get away. Neil and I were to be the men on this trip. That was why my mother had let me come along, to help Neil drive and to keep him company. It was the summer of 1952, when I was fifteen and so was he.

We'd come right up the spine of Arkansas from East Texas, winding through the Ouachita and Ozark Mountains on U.S. Highway 71. We wanted to make Kansas City before midnight. Mrs. Pomeroy had packed plenty of sandwiches and some fruit, but around sundown, just south of Fayetteville, we decided to stop for pie, and to give our legs a stretch.

I won't name the town. But it was stuck on a mountainside and had just a single main street. There were two cafes, though, facing each other across the street. I don't remember their names so I'll call them the Gem and the Star. Since I was their guest, the Pomeroys let me pick which one—and I chose the Star.

When we entered, the place was empty except for a middle-aged woman behind the cash register. There was a counter with about a dozen stools and along the opposite wall a row of booths. Ceiling fans turned slowly overhead. We selected a booth toward the back and the woman brought over four glasses of water on a tray.

"What'll y'all have?" she said.

Mrs. Pomeroy ordered coffee with her pie, and Neil and I ordered milk with ours. Carol Kay decided she didn't want pie and ordered an ice cream sundae instead. The woman went away and returned shortly with our order on another tray.

While we were eating, three men came in and sat down at the counter. Two of them were probably in their twenties (though they seemed older than that to me then, at fifteen) and the other was about forty or so, I'd say. Old enough to be an uncle to the other two. They ordered coffee and sat there on their stools with their backs to us, drinking it.

When Mrs. Pomeroy finished her pie, she excused herself and went back to the ladies' room in the rear of the café. Over at the counter, the young man nearest us turned on his stool to watch her go. Then he said something to the other young man, beside him. They laughed, and the second man spun all the way around on his stool until he was facing us. He eyed us for a moment, grinning, then spoke.

"Where y'all from?"

We stared at him from our booth. We didn't know whether to answer him or not. Finally, Neil told him we were from Marshall, Texas.

"Where you headed?"

"Kansas City, Missourah," Neil said proudly.

"Ka-a-a-nsas City," the man said, dragging it out. "Whatchall gonna do up there?"

By this time the other two men had spun around on their stools too and were grinning at us. The older man had some teeth missing.

"Visit my aunt and uncle," Neil said. "They live up there."

"Say they do?" the man said. "Well, I'll be God damn. Who's that there in the booth with you?"

Neil hesitated, then gave the men our names. By this

time Carol Kay had her hands in her lap and was staring into her ice cream dish. I glanced up toward the woman at the cash register, but she was gazing out the plate glass front window, paying no attention to us.

"Carol Kay, huh?" the man said. "She your sister?"

Neil nodded.

"How old is she?"

Neil hesitated again. "Twelve."

"Is that all?" the interrogator said. "She looks right big for twelve."

Neil didn't say anything. The man whispered something to the young man beside him and they both laughed again. Then the man in the middle whispered to the older man and he laughed too.

Just then Mrs. Pomeroy returned from the ladies' room. She looked at the men at the counter, all three of whom were still facing our way, still grinning, then slid back into the booth beside Carol Kay.

"Well, now," she said brightly. "Is everyone about finished?"

None of us said anything. My pie was only half-eaten, and so was Neil's. Carol Kay's sundae was largely intact too, though it was starting to melt. I stared down at my plate. My appetite had deserted me. It had completely gone away.

"You the mama?" a voice said.

Mrs. Pomeroy bent her attention to us. "Let's finish up now," she said. "We've still got a long way to go."

Everyone tried to address their food. But Neil and Carol Kay were like me and we all just picked at it.

"Hey, mama," the voice said again. "All them kids yours? You don't look old enough to have all them kids."

"Eat your ice cream, Carol Kay," Mrs. Pomeroy said. "Don't you need to go to the restroom? If you do, you'd better hurry. We're leaving here soon."

"She look old enough to have all them kids to you, Riley?" the voice said.

"Naw," a second voice said. "She don't look near old enough to me."

"How about you, Thurl?" the first voice said. "She look old enough to you?"

"Shit, no," a third voice said. "I don't even think they're hers."

"How old a woman would you say she was?"

"Oh, thirty, thirty-two—somewhere in there. Just that *good* age."

The other two laughed.

"Come on, kids," Mrs. Pomeroy said, rising from the booth. "Just leave it. We're getting out of here."

The three of us scrambled out of the booth after her, and with Mrs. Pomeroy leading the way, headed for the front of the café. But the man on the middle of the three stools stood up in the aisle, blocking our path.

"Hey, now," he said. "What's y'all's hurry? Missy there didn't finish her cream yet. Them boys ain't eat their pie."

We four stood pressed together in the narrow aisle between the booths and the row of stools. The man blocking our way was large and broad-shouldered, and he showed no intention of moving aside to let us pass. The other two were still on their stools, looking up at us.

"What's a matter, Missy?" the one on the first stool said, poking a toe at Carol Kay. "You lose your appetite? Big girl like you don't eat, she won't fill out proper."

I could see Carol Kay out of the corner of my eye. Her face was all clenched up and she looked like she was about to cry. I had begun to shake uncontrollably and was afraid I might cry too.

"Let us through, please," I heard Mrs. Pomeroy say. "You've frightened the children. I think that's enough."

She attempted to move around the man standing in the aisle, but the man moved with her, blocking her way again.

"Aw, now, mama," he said. "What's your hurry?"

"Please get out of my way," Mrs. Pomeroy said.

The man looked at his seated friends. "I believe she wants by. Whadda y'all think? Should I let her?"

There was silence for a moment. Overhead the fans turned. It was the older man who finally spoke.

"Aster for a little kiss first."

The first man grinned. "A kiss? You think I should?"

"Yeah. Aster for a little kiss."

The man in the aisle looked at Mrs. Pomeroy. "Hear that, ma'am? He thinks I ought to ast you for a kiss. What would you say to that?"

Mrs. Pomeroy didn't say anything. She stood very still, her arms down at her sides. The rest of us were right behind her, bunched tight.

"One little smooch—then you can be on your way."

The man in the aisle began lowering his large, heavy face toward Mrs. Pomeroy.

Neil was right in front of me. "Hey…," I heard him say, sort of under his breath.

The man's big face continued toward Mrs. Pomeroy.

"One little smooch," he said again.

Carol Kay was crying now, and I was on the verge of it. Neil was squirming in front of me, acting as if he wanted to do something but couldn't decide what.

"I'll scream," I heard Mrs. Pomeroy say. "If you come any closer, so help me God I'll scream."

The man's big face widened in another grin. "Hear that, Riley? She's gonna scream."

"Oo-ee," Riley said. "She's one a them, is she? Well, tell her to let fly."

He had pushed himself up off his stool by now and was standing beside Mrs. Pomeroy. He wasn't much taller than she was. He whispered something in her ear.

Mrs. Pomeroy was wearing a blue sun dress that left her shoulders bare. I could see them start to redden.

"I mean it," she said, her voice rising. "I'll scream."

"She's fixin' to, Riley!" the man in front said. "She's

fixin' to! We better git our kiss while we can."

He raised his big, thick-fingered hands, and was about to take Mrs. Pomeroy by the shoulders—or so it seemed to me—when a sharp voice from the front of the café brought everything to a standstill.

"*That's enough, Monroe.*"

It was the woman behind the cash register. She was looking back in our direction now, and not out the window, though she hadn't moved from her spot. There was enough authority in her voice, however, even from there, to deflate our tormentors. Suddenly they became like small boys: resentful, a bit recalcitrant at first, but unwilling, finally, to challenge the grownup in the room. Amid an amount of grousing and foot scuffing they returned to their stools and their cooling coffees and let us be on our way.

As we paid our bill up front, the woman said, as if nothing at all had happened, "Was everything okay?"

"Fine," Mrs. Pomeroy said, collaborating in the fiction. "Everything was fine."

"Well, y'all come on back then, you hear?" the woman said as we went out the door.

It was my turn to drive, and I got us quickly out of that town and back on the highway headed north. We were very quiet in the car for a number of miles, each of us occupied, I suppose, with our own thoughts. I couldn't look at Neil, and he couldn't look at me. We sat there in the front seat together pretending a consuming interest in what we were seeing out the windshield. After a while Mrs. Pomeroy spoke to us. She said we weren't to feel bad about what had happened. She said we should just forget about it, because that was what she was going to do. "Once we get to Kansas City," she assured us, "it won't amount to a hill of beans."

I wanted to believe her, but it was hard to. What had happened *was* important, it seemed to me. There had been powerful forces at work back there in that café, I felt, forces that, at fifteen, I still didn't know nearly enough about. They weren't exactly *evil* forces, I sensed, just very powerful ones—and very dangerous. The kind of thing that could get a person killed.

And despite what she'd said, I understood that Mrs. Pomeroy knew all this better than I did, and wouldn't soon be forgetting what had happened either.

# FOOTBALL

When I think about the happiest moments of my life, as I sometimes do now that I've reached the summing-up age of seventy, I find I often skip over the more obvious ones like Wedding Day, and Birth of First Child, and so forth, and go directly to certain autumn Saturday mornings outside the Cotton Bowl in Dallas when I was seventeen. There's a tingle of excitement in the air on these mornings, together with the kind of crispness that doesn't arrive in Texas until late October, and I'm here with several of my Marshall High School teammates, standing in the pre-game crowd, and we are on display.

We will have played our own game of football the night before, back in Marshall, some hundred and fifty miles to the east, and coming to Dallas—being driven there, usually, by someone's father—for a big-time college game, Baylor against SMU, say, or Oklahoma against Texas, is a part of our reward. Our exertions on behalf of Marshall have earned this for us; we know that, and are more than comfortable with it. We're looking forward to the game, of course—that's part of the tingle in the air—but make no mistake about it, we're there primarily to be *seen*.

And as we look around outside the Cotton Bowl we observe other little clumps of high school teammates similar to ourselves, and we understand that that's the main reason they're there too. We check out their letterjackets, just as they are checking out ours. That bunch over there in the black and gold jackets, for example, with the big block G's on their left breasts. Gladewater? Gainesville? And those guys off to our right in the flashy purple numbers with the white leather sleeves. Paschal, out of Fort Worth? Or Lufkin? If it's Lufkin, well, hey, we played those guys just a couple of weeks ago! Maybe we ought to saunter over and rehash the game. *Aren't you that number 71 that kept jamming up the middle on us? Aren't you the number 33 that caught that pass on the fake punt play?*

It's like a ritual gathering of the tribes, those Saturday mornings out front of the Cotton Bowl. We have come there from all over the northern half of the state. We represent our towns. Those big block letters on our chests say so. It has been suggested to us more than once by now that we are the flower of these towns' youth, whether it's Marshall, or Gainesville, or Lufkin. And by now we have no trouble at all believing it.

We pose, we strut, we preen. If there's been an injury to one of us, all the better. A slight limp is our equivalent of the Croix de Guerre. This was in the days before face masks, and any kind of facial cut or scratch will have been daubed with iodine to increase its visibility. Stitches? The more the better. Stitches are signs of true nobility. (As if such signs were needed!)

Several years ago I was watching on TV the observances of the fiftieth anniversary of the D-Day landings at Normandy. Much of the coverage was extremely moving to anyone of my generation, with dim childhood memories of the events depicted, and occasionally I found myself fighting back tears. There was one moment when the tears won, though, and my wife came into the room to find me bawling. When she asked why, I had trouble explaining it to her.

They'd been showing some old newsreel footage of General Eisenhower talking to a group of American paratroopers just hours before the invasion. Ike—an old football player himself—was moving among the men, shaking hands with some, joking with others, in an atmosphere of camaraderie and mutual respect; you could tell they liked each other. All the men, except for Ike, looked very young, no more than teenagers some of them. And gradually I began to notice, as I watched them grinning and chatting with their commander there on the screen, that a number of them, more than just one or two, had shaved their heads, all except for a center scalplock, in a style that used to be known, in less politically correct days, as a Mohawk.

It was the sight of all those Mohawks that brought the tears to my eyes and wouldn't let them stop coming. Such an American thing to do! So *jock*! We'd shaved our heads just like that the night before the Kilgore game!

The paratroopers Ike was talking to, it turns out, were members of the so-called "pathfinders" group whose job it was to jump ahead of the regular airborne units that night and lead the way to certain key targets behind the lines in France. They suffered eighty percent casualties. Some had the misfortune to jump into a field where the Germans were holding night anti-aircraft exercises. I have this vivid mental image of a German officer examining the bodies of some of these American dead, seeing those Mohawk haircuts, and being puzzled.

"*Indianer?*" he says to the man beside him, his adjutant.

"*Weiss nicht,*" the adjutant says. "Who knows what these crazy Americans will do?"

I first started playing (or trying to play) organized football at age twelve, in the seventh grade. I stood about five-two at the time and weighed approximately eighty pounds. The team I was trying to make was called the Marshall Junior High School Mighty Mites, and I didn't succeed in making it. I was bigger the next year, though, at five-four and nearly ninety pounds, and I did make the team. But I didn't letter. A fact that so crushed me that nearly twenty years later I wrote a short story about it called

"Win a Few, Lose a Few" that was published in the old *Saturday Evening Post*.

It was in spring training following that fall of not lettering, though, that I finally made a place for myself in Marshall's football thinking. (Yes. Spring training. In junior high school. This was Texas, after all.) What happened was that during a scrimmage with the high school "B" team the coaches put me in on defense at one point and I managed to make a series of tackles, one after the other, on a big, bow-legged country boy named Doyle McQueen. I still only weighed about ninety pounds, and Doyle must have weighed nearly twice that. But they kept running him at me, and by diving low and hitting him around the ankles, I kept bringing him down. It probably only happened two or three times, but in memory, over fifty years later, it seems like half a dozen. And, thus, instantly, my reputation was made.

"He"—meaning me—"may not be very big," all the coaches began to say, "but that little scamp'll hit you. He'll get after you."

Soon I was hearing it all over town. "He's a hitter, that little scamp. He can bring those big boys down."

I lettered my final year in junior high school, as a 114-pound defensive back, and then went on to letter all three years in high school. Mostly I played in the defensive backfield in high school too, as a sort of rover whose job it was to line up opposite where we thought the play might be going. The position required me to make a lot of tackles, but I didn't mind. It was what I was good at. As a senior, I stood six feet tall and weighed 170 pounds, which was considered big in those days.

I also played football briefly in junior college, up at Paris, Texas, before having a run-in with the coach and then flunking out of school. My last two years of organized ball were in the Marines. I played for my battalion team at Twentynine Palms, out in the California desert, and in both years was a member of the Twentynine Palms All-Stars, who traveled around to other bases—Barstow, El Toro, and the like—for games. I wrote a short story about getting banged up in one of those games that was published a few years ago in one of the literary quarterlies. The game was against the Barstow Marines, up at Barstow, and I got hurt trying to stop an end sweep. It was Doyle McQueen all over again, only this time I didn't get low enough and the runner's knees came up and caught me flush in the mouth. I woke up on the sidelines. It took a dozen stitches to put my lower lip back together. This happened on November 10, 1957. I know the date because November 10 is the Marine Corps' birthday, and there was a dance going on in the gym when we got back down to Twentynine Palms that evening. I can still remember being shunned, because of my bandaged lip, by all the girls who'd been bussed out from LA to serve as dance partners.

I last put on a pair of shoulder pads in the fall of 1958, when I was 22, for a game against the El Toro Marines. It was a hot day out in the desert, our kind of weather, and we won the game, but I don't remember the score. All told, I spent parts of nine years playing organized football. And I continued to fantasize about playing after that. As an undergraduate down at the University of Texas after I got out of the Marines, I toyed, I can recall, with the idea of trying out for the varsity team as a "walk-on." This was during the Darrell Royal era, however, when the Texas Longhorns were contending for the national championship every year, and I finally decided they were doing okay without me.

Over the years I have continued to be an avid fan of football, following the fortunes of the Longhorns and the Dallas Cowboys and the Vikings here in Minnesota, where I now live. I've watched the game change for the better and for the worse. The players are better protected now, and better trained, but they're also bigger and faster, and they hit each other with greater force. A major change has been the way black athletes have come to dominate the game. Marshall's schools were segregated when I played; we were just a bunch of slow-footed little white boys running around out there. Now the Marshall team—which won a state championship not long ago—is virtually all black. It's doubtful that any of us who played back in the days of segregation could even have made today's teams. The Texas Longhorns were also all-white (at Darrell Royal's insistence) when I was there, back in the early sixties, and now they too are mostly black. As is the National Football League, where something over seventy percent of current players are African-American.

Carl Lewis, the former Olympic sprinter and long jumper, was asked some years back for his thoughts on why black athletes have risen to such dominance in almost all sports in recent years.

"We appear to be put together better," he said.

Maybe. But we'll see.

I first started having trouble with my back about twenty-five years ago, when I was working at the state capitol in St. Paul. I reached down to return a racquetball serve one noontime during a game with a fellow worker and felt a sudden sharp pain at the base of my spine and running all the way down my right leg to my heel. It was as if there was a red hot poker, or, worse yet, a live electric wire, inside my leg. It hurt like hell. I had never experienced anything like that before.

It went away after a while, though, and I forgot about it. But then it happened again, a year or so later, as I was helping a friend push a car out of a snowbank one wintry night in Minneapolis. Same electric surge down the right leg. Same excruciating pain. I went to my HMO doctor and had it diagnosed.

Sciatica, I was told. I was suffering from sciatica.

Now, I had always associated sciatica in my mind with the elderly, although I hadn't known exactly what it was. To me, it was one of those comic-sounding words for a minor, also faintly comic, medical condition: eczema, psoriasis, sciatica. Turns out there's something called the sciatic nerve that runs all the way down the spine, and then on down the right leg. Sciatica is simply the term for a bruising, and subsequent inflammation, of this nerve. The HMO nurse gave me some muscle relaxants, told me to stay off my feet for a few days, and sent me home.

Again the pain went away after a while and I went back to doing the things I'd been doing, including playing racquetball. Every now and then the pain would return, though, for no immediate reason that I was aware of, and I would have to take it easy for a few days until it let up. This went on for a number of years, with the pain recurring, lingering for a short time, and then going away. This, I decided, was what it meant to "have" sciatica. I would just have to learn to live with it.

But then about ten years ago the pain showed up again, and this time it didn't go away. It has been with me more or less constantly ever since. It's not excruciating—not yet, anyway—but it's almost always there. So much so that I can no longer wear a belt and have to use suspenders to hold up my pants. And my pants have to be two sizes too large in the waist to lessen their rubbing against my damaged nerves. I wear sweatpants, with a very loose drawstring, around the house these days, and when I sit down it's in a chair with extra cushions. I'm advised to take painkillers and to use heat ointments, as needed, which is turning out to be distressingly often.

When it became apparent to me that the pain wasn't going to go away this time, I went back to my HMO doctor and he ordered a CAT scan. The CAT scan showed that I have a degenerative arthritic condition all up and down my spine, which has resulted—is resulting—in a narrowing of the channel through which both my spinal cord and my sciatic nerve travel. It's this narrowing of the channel that's keeping the nerve more or less constantly bruised and inflamed these days. The condition is common enough that it even has a name: *spinal stenosis*.

One of the first things the doctor said to me, as he held my CAT scan up to the light to show me what he was talking about, was, "Did you play football as a kid?"

When I answered him, he said, "I thought so," then proceeded to tell me what we were looking at.

Those calcium deposits—which are what arthritis is—around my spinal discs were the spine's way of trying to cushion itself from the traumatic shock of all the blocking and tackling I did as a kid. If I wanted to I could probably label the deposits as they appear on my CAT scan. Here's "Doyle McQueen," for instance, right up here at the top. And here, down quite a bit lower, is that son of a bitch from Barstow who busted my lip before running right over me.

*Spinal stenosis.* How many other men in America my age or older suffer from it, I wonder. The American brand of football is a game you play with your shoulders. That's why they give you those big shoulder pads. And every block and every tackle a football player makes, if he does it right, sends a little calcium-coated message to his spine. *Danger! Stop it! Don't do that!* Now that young black men are so preponderant in the playing of the game, will spinal stenosis be added to their collective etiology, along with sickle-cell anemia and high blood pressure and diabetes, when they reach my age? I wonder.

I still watch football on TV—the Vikings, the Super Bowl, an occasional college game—but as I do so I can't help cringing now, after a particularly brutal hit, at the thought of what these players must be doing to their spines. As has been remarked elsewhere, more than once, the American version of the game of football is almost eerily reflective of certain of our national characteristics: the violence, the patterned (as opposed to freeform) nature of the play, the emphasis on such things as strategy and logistics. We Americans are said to be geniuses at logistics, an attribute that served us well in World War Two, when we were always able to bring to bear, whether at Normandy or Iwo Jima or anywhere else, more men and equipment than our enemies. American football is premised on that very notion: of arriving at the "point of attack," whether on an end sweep or a plunge up the middle, with more personnel than the opposing side. And it's often this circumstance, the moment when the three seek to overwhelm the two, or the two the one, that brings on injuries. It's how I got obliterated up at Barstow that day, hurling myself headlong in front of all those churning knees.

So what, finally, is there to say? Given the current condition of my spine, should I rue the day I first put on a pair of shoulder pads? The day I first stepped out onto that practice field down at the old city park in long-ago Marshall, Texas? And if I had known then what I know now, would I do it all over again?

These are hard questions for me to answer. They're even hard questions for me to ask. Neither of my two sons played football—though one did give hockey a brief try—and for this I think I'm glad. I *think* I'm glad. Neither served in the Marine Corps either, or in any other branch of the service, and I think I'm glad about that too. But it does sometimes seem to me that maybe they have missed something. Some ineffable—something.

Because, like I say, when I think back over the happiest moments of my life, I very quickly go to those mornings outside the Cotton Bowl so many years ago. I can see us there so clearly, can all but smell that special autumn freshness in the air. We've got our letterjackets on, with the collars turned up for a James Dean effect, and our Levis are riding low on our slim and powerful hips. We're so utterly alive, so filled with blood and energy, that our feet just barely touch the ground. We're Marshall, Texas's best, by God—if not as a group its very brightest—and we're there in Dallas on parade, for all the envying world to see.

# Youth

*It is dawn and we are coming up out of Mexico* in Neil's old black Ford. I'm driving and he's resting his head against the glass on the passenger side. We've just spent a riotous night in Nuevo Laredo, frolicking among the bar girls and *mariachis*, and now we're headed back to East Texas. I am home on leave from the Marines and this is the happiest I've been in months. What makes me happy, of course, is that I'm with Neil. He's my best friend—has been since the fifth grade—and I consider myself his, although he did sign his Most Popular Boy picture in my high school yearbook two years ago, "To one of my best friends," a fact that still rankles a little when I think about it. What's this "one of" marlarkey, Neil? I want to ask him.

"Hey," I say to him now. "You asleep?"

He lifts his head. "I was," he says, "until just a second ago."

"What woke you?"

"You did, asking me if I was asleep."

"Oh."

He sits up, yawns prodigiously and smacks his lips. "You got any gum?" he says. "My mouth tastes like the Russian cavalry just rode through it and the last horse defecated."

I fish in my shirt pocket and come up with some Chiclets, which a little Mexican kid sold me outside the Papagayo Club at two in the morning. I hand them to him.

He opens the tiny container and pops them into his mouth.

"Be gone you pesky Russians."

I'm having trouble keeping my own eyes open. We haven't really slept since I arrived in Austin on Saturday and Neil picked me up at the bus depot. That was three days ago. He was finishing up his summer school classes at the University of Texas; the Ford's backseat is filled now with his clothes and books and other belongings. Mexico was his idea. Neil always has all the good ideas, is always the first to seize on any new chance for adventure.

We drive in silence for a while. We're on that barren stretch of highway between Laredo and Pearsall. There's not another car in forty miles. The sun is just coming up off to our right, throwing an interesting mix of light and shadow across the sea of mesquite and prickly pear we're moving through.

"I could use a little pick-me-up," Neil says. "How about you?"

He means a drink, of course, and despite the fact that we're some sixty-odd hours into an epic debauch, this takes on the immediate stature of a good idea. We're young, after all. Our bodies are marvelous metabolic machines. Toxins fly out of us like pigeons out of a magician's hat.

"Don't mind if I do," I say, and Neil leans over and begins digging around in his clothes on the backseat. After a moment he comes up with a full bottle of Jim Beam, which he uncaps and we begin passing back and forth between us.

We proceed up Highway 81 this way, nipping at the Jim Beam and watching the sun come up over Texas. It is the summer of 1958 and, like I say, I am the happiest I've been in months.

*What is it about some people that makes them, almost from the moment they can walk and talk, the object of all eyes? There used to be a word for this, cynosure, but you don't see it used much anymore. Hoby Baker, the hockey player and all-around athlete, was said to be such a figure for Scott Fitzgerald and his crowd at Princeton in the days before World War I. Fitzgerald, lamenting his own lack of it, termed the quality Baker possessed "animal magnetism," and went to his grave envying him for it.*

In my hometown of Marshall, Texas, in the years when I was growing up there, among my peers and classmates the person who filled this role for us was Neil Pomeroy. He was our golden one. He was the one who represented for us, we felt, the best expression of our collective selves.

I first met Neil at South Side Elementary School, after transferring over there from East End Elementary. The boy we'd all looked up to at East End had been a stocky littler scrapper named Tubby Eubanks, and I'd sort of hoped to be that boy myself when I enrolled at South Side. But as soon as I saw Neil I knew I didn't stand a chance. His luminosity far outshone Tubby Eubanks's. I was going to have to settle for being a sidekick, playing second or third fiddle, again.

In A Separate Peace, John Knowles describes that novel's golden boy, a prep school adolescent whom he calls Phineas, as possessing "an extra vigor, a heightened confidence in himself, a serene capacity for affection…" He speaks of Phineas's "harmonious and natural unity." And all of these traits come close, but only close, it seems to me, to explaining Neil's effect on people. He expected to be liked. He expected you to defer to him because you would just naturally want to. And he was right! He was president of every class he ever found himself in, captain of every team. Most Popular Boy. Most Likely To Succeed. Most Whatever He Chose To Be Most Of.

His parents weren't well-to-do—his father managed the local telephone company—but they doted on him too, giving him just about anything he ever wanted. It was as if they realized they had been lucky enough to bring someone special into their midst and they didn't want to risk screwing it up. He had a younger sister named Carol Kay and she early on learned to be content just to stand aside and watch. It was my good luck, from the fifth grade on, to live just down the street from Neil. This gave me increased access and stood me in good stead when we went off to junior high and high school. Because people saw us together so often they more or less assumed we were best friends, that ours was a special relationship. And I, for my part, let them assume it.

Just before he went away to the University of Texas, where he would pledge one of the best fraternities and hobnob with some of the wealthiest boys in the state, his parents, having scrimped and saved for months to do *so, presented him with a car to get around in. It was a used car, though, a two-door Ford that was several years old already, and they seemed to be somewhat apologetic about this, as if to say, "We hope we haven't let you down here, Neil. We hope you won't mind driving this."*

*That's the car he and I were coming up out of Mexico in that day.*

By mid-morning we're just south of Waco and the bottle of Jim Beam, now resting on the seat between us, is half empty. We've also stopped at a convenience store outside San Antonio and picked up a six pack of Pearl beer, some sticks of beef jerky, and about a dozen pickled hard boiled eggs. The sun is well up in the sky by now, the temperature already in the mid-eighties, and we've got every window in the car rolled down. We are wide awake and tearing up the highway. It's great to be alive.

Suddenly we see a hitchhiker up ahead, a solitary figure with his thumb out. Neil is driving now. He begins to brake immediately and soon we're skidding to a halt on the road's gravel shoulder, just past where the hitchhiker stands.

He is at the window quickly and I'm opening the passenger door and leaning forward to let him into the backseat.

"Just push that junk out of the way back there," Neil tells him. "Make yourself at home."

The hitchhiker is a young man about our age, maybe twenty or twenty-one. He is wearing khaki shorts and hiking boots and is carrying a small canvas knapsack. We can tell he's not from around here even before he opens his mouth. Nobody in Texas wears shorts or boots like those, or carries a knapsack like that.

"Where you headed?" Neil says, getting us back up on the road.

"Just north," the boy says. "Anywhere north is fine."

"Where you coming from?" I say.

"I was down in Mexico."

"Yeah? So were we. Where in Mexico?"

The boy then tells us a tale of traveling by motorbike—not

motor*cycle*, motor*bike*—from New Orleans, where he'd bought the thing, all the way down to Brownsville and then on into Mexico as far south as the Yucatan before it finally fell apart on him ("Too many mountains; too many bad roads.") outside of Merida. He sold it for junk there, he says, took a series of buses back up to the border, eventually, and started hitchhiking. We're his third ride. He has to be back in New Haven, Connecticut, in time for fall classes, he says, but otherwise he's loose as a goose, though a bit broke.

"You look kinda thirsty," Neil says. "Could you use a beer?"

The boy grins. "Hey, I sure could. But isn't it against the law, drinking and driving?"

"Nah," Neil says. "Not really. Not unless they catch you."

I open a beer with the church key and hand it back to him. He takes a sip and says, "Aah. Nectar of the gods."

"You want a pickled egg?" I say.

He looks at me as if he's trying to decide whether I'm serious or not: apparently pickled eggs aren't standard fare where he comes from. But, "Sure," he says. "Why not?"

We're doing about seventy now, just hammering through the heart of Texas. The world is our playpen and everything we pass is simply one more sign of an approving God. "Whee!" Neil says at one point. "Wonder what the *poor* folks are doing!"

After a few more miles of this we come to the big overhead sign announcing an approaching divide in the highway, one fork leading to Dallas-Fort Worth and the other to Corsicana and the rest of East Texas.

"Decision time!" Neil shouts. "Which will it be, gents? Anyone got a preference?"

"Dallas!" I say, taking my cue from Neil's tone. "I've already *been* home."

"How about you, Lowell?" That's the name of the boy in the backseat. By this time I've noticed that he has a slightly deformed left hand. It's smaller than the other one, and a couple of the fingers seem stiff. Neil has noticed it too, I suspect, and partly as a result has taken a real shine to Lowell. I know him well enough to know his thinking: anyone who can ride a motorbike from New Orleans to the Yucatan, especially with a hand like that, is not to be gainsaid.

"Oh, Dallas, definitely," Lowell says, entering into the spirit of things. "I'd be a fool to come all the way to Texas and not see Big D."

The result is that some time later we find ourselves seated on stools in the Town Pump Tavern in the fancy Highland Park section of North Dallas, not far from Southern Methodist University, the state's (some would say nation's) premiere party school. The place is nearly empty when we arrive, but before long it begins to fill up with the kind of fresh-faced fraternity and sorority types one always associates with SMU. There are lots of madras shorts and button-down short sleeve shirts. Some of the girls are knockouts. Neil, whose own fraternity down in Austin has a strong SMU chapter, seems to know at least half of the people in the room—and everyone, of course, adores him.

He tells them all about Lowell's adventure, making Lowell the center of attention for a while, and by nightfall the good fellowship in the Town Pump is so thick you could wrap and package it. Everybody loves Lowell. Everybody loves Neil. Everybody loves *me!* We have brought a breath of something new (Lowell) to the comfortable boredom of Highland Park and, at least for the evening, we can do no wrong. Girls vie for our attention. Lowell, with his East Coast accent and his air of vulnerability, is a particular hit. Neil and I get dragooned for a party out in Arlington, and the last we see of Lowell, as we head out the door around midnight, he's up on a table at the back of the bar doing some kind of wild Cossack dance to the rhythmic clapping of about a dozen pretty coeds.

Outside, as we prepare to follow the caravan setting out for Arlington, we discover Lowell's knapsack still in the backseat of Neil's car. We take it out and sit it on the curb, leaning it carefully against a parking meter so he'll be sure to see it when he comes out.

*What causes a bright flame to suddenly gutter and go out? I've thought about this a good deal in regard to Neil, and my conclusion is that maybe some people are just born to be a certain age and no more. John Keats died at twenty-five, for instance. Try to picture Keats as an old man. Or James Dean, dead at twenty-six. Can anyone imagine a middle-aged James Dean? Elvis died physically at forty-two, but by that time he was just a shell. The real Elvis, the one the world wants to remember, was a swivel-hipped youngster in his twenties, with energy to burn.*

*Something happened to Neil in his thirties and I'm still not sure what it was. But by a decade or so after that night at the Town Pump in Highland Park he was a changed man. He'd gone to law school after finishing up at UT, and, taking the first job offered to him out of law school, had wound up as the county attorney of a small, rural jurisdiction back up in East Texas. There, he married, began a family, joined the nearest country club, and settled in.*

*In the meantime, I myself had gone off to UT after the Marines, and then on to graduate school in the Midwest and a brief career in college teaching, before eventually winding up working as a policy analyst for the legislature up in Minnesota.*

*My contact with Neil during this time had been fitful and fleeting, and my next strong memory of him centers on another night in another bar in Dallas in the mid-70's. I'd come down to monitor a mass transit conference for the Minnesota Senate and had made arrangements to meet for a drink with another old high school classmate, a fellow named Vernon Watts, who was fast rising in the management hierarchy at Ling-Temco-Vought, the big defense contractor out in Grand Prairie. Neil learned about our plans from Vernon and decided to drive over the sixty or so miles from his little East Texas base of operations at Canton to join us.*

*It was an interesting evening. There we were in the cocktail lounge of the Hyatt Regency in downtown Dallas: three young men in their mid-thirties, properly suited and tied, reasonably affluent, enjoying good health, riding the latest wave of U.S. empire. Anyone looking on would have viewed us as classic late-twentieth-century American types—a government operative, an arms dealer, and a small town lawyer—and basically they*

*would have been right. Except that they could not have known Neil, our*
*comet, our shooting star, as he used to be.*

*Superficially he was still the same. The grin was still there, the strong*
*handshake, the self-confident veneer. But just beneath the surface, you could*
*tell, something was beginning to give way. That bright inner light hadn't*
*gone out yet, but it was getting dimmer. We ended up in a country-western*
*bar out on the Jacksboro Strip that evening in the company of some young*
*women who'd attached themselves to us, for reasons of their own, back at*
*the Hyatt. Throughout the evening Neil seemed both a part and not a*
*part of the festivities, and when it came time to split up back in the Hyatt*
*parking lot he discovered that he'd lost his car keys. This was so unlike*
*Neil, the haplessness of it, the futility, that I remember being struck by it*
*even then. We searched all over for his keys but never found them, and in*
*the end Vernon had to drive him all the way home to Canton in Vernon's*
*car. I went along to keep Vernon company on the way back. Neil sat*
*in the backseat and brooded the whole way. We let him out outside his*
*house at three in the morning and sat watching as, slump-shouldered, he*
*approached his own front door like a man going to his doom. I wouldn't*
*see him again after that for a number of years.*

But now it's dawn again in that summer of '58 and
we're heading east in Neil's old Ford from the party house in
Arlington. In fact we're nearly home; we've long since put
Dallas and its sinful pleasures behind us and are making our
way, stoplight by stoplight, through Longview on Highway 80,
just twenty miles west of Marshall.

"How you feeling, tiger?" Neil says from behind the wheel,
and I have to admit to him that I'm dragging. We have been up
all night again, our heads scarcely touching a pillow. The party
in Arlington had been something of a disappointment—the
girls flighty and disinterested, people bailing out around four,
a certain amount of nausea and vomiting coming into play—
but, hey, you can't win 'em all.

"I could use a little dip," Neil says. "How about you?"

"A dip?" I'm not sure what he means. It's about six
o'clock in the morning, after all, and we're in the middle of a

highway.

"Yeah," Neil says. "I don't think I'm gonna make it otherwise. My eyes keep wanting to close."

"I know what you mean," I say. "Mine too."

We're stopped at a red light on the eastern edge of Longview, having just about negotiated a ten-mile strip of service stations, barbecue joints, gun shops, real estate offices, oilfield supply lots, and motels. Up ahead on our right is the darkened neon sign, a huge electric display when lit, of the Dun Roamin' Inn, probably Longview's premiere lodgings, certainly its gaudiest, of the era.

"Let's do it then," Neil says, and when the light changes he drives forward the necessary quarter mile or so and turns in at the Dun Roamin' Inn. He eases the old black Ford through the overhanging archway and past the manager's office and brings us to a stop in an unoccupied parking space outside one of the lower rental units. We are in the big motel's inner courtyard. Rising up all around us, three stories high, are the temporary sleeping quarters of dozens of weary travelers. Out in the middle of the courtyard, past the slides and the swing set, is a big, Olympic-style pool, with both a low and a high diving board. Umbrella-shaded tables ring its perimeter.

"Last one in's an Aggie cheerleader," Neil says. He is already out of the car and taking his shirt off. He strips all the way down to his jockey shorts, leaving everything there on the hood of the car, and sets out across the courtyard at a rapid clip. I strip down to my Marine skivvies and set out after him.

"Yippee!" Neil shouts, doing a belly flop off the low board.

"Yahoo!" I shout, coming in right after him.

The water temperature is maybe seventy degrees and it feels great. It wakes us right up. Soon we're doing laps and splashing one another. A traveler comes out of one of the rooms up on the third floor and begins making his way downstairs. He pauses on the second landing and looks out at us. He has on a suit and tie and is carrying a clothes bag and a big sample kit. A salesman of some kind, no doubt.

"How's the water?" he shouts.

"Not bad!" we say. "Come on in."

"Shit," he says. "Don't I wish."

After a few minutes the night clerk, a teenaged boy, comes out of the office up front and stands at the edge of the pool. He watches us for a moment, then says, "Uh, are y'all registered here?"

Neil tells him nope, we're just passing through. And when the boy, looking puzzled, hesitates, Neil tells him we're trying to win a bet by swimming in every motel pool between Dallas and the Louisiana line. The Dun Roamin's is our fifteenth so far, he tells him, and we still have five to go.

"Damn," the boy says. "That's a lot of pools." He thinks for a moment, then adds, "Be careful of that Best Western in Hallsville. I hear it's got a fungus."

We say we will, and a short time later we're back on the road again, refreshed, cruising on home to Marshall in our wet underwear.

*The last time I saw Neil alive was the winter of 1986. I had gone home to Marshall to be with my mother who was in failing health and wouldn't make it to the new year. Neil drove over from Canton and we had dinner together at the home of a couple of former high school classmates. Neil didn't look good. He'd put on weight and his color was bad. Pasty. He tried to be the old Neil for us, but you could tell his heart wasn't in it. One of his daughters was beginning to make a name for herself as a fashion model in New York and he seemed reasonably pleased about that, but for the most part he was sluggish, morose. The conversation at the dinner table and in the living room afterwards seemed to go right by him. We left the dinner party early, with him driving, and all the way back to my mother's place he complained peevishly about this and that: his wife's spending habits, his youngest son's taste in television shows, and so on. Little things. Inconsequential. He sounded for all the world like a crotchety old man. When he let me out of the car we said a brief goodbye to each other and I never saw him again.*

*About eight months later the ex-classmate who had hosted the dinner that night called me in Minneapolis, where I live, to say that Neil had died. Heart attack, he said. He'd come out of the bathroom the night before there at his home in Canton, complained to his wife about not feeling well, had sat down on their bed to catch his breath, lay back, and quietly expired. He was fifty-one years old.*

It is three days after our early-morning dip in the Dun Roamin' Inn's pool. Neil and I are sitting out on the front porch of his parents' house on Garrett Street, bouncing a tennis ball back and forth between us the way we used to do. My leave is just about up; I'll be boarding a Greyhound bus the next morning for the long ride back to the Marine base at Twentynine Palms, California.

Suddenly Marshall's lone taxicab pulls up out front of the house and someone we think we recognize hops out. It's Lowell. He's come looking for his knapsack.

After we greet him and ask him how he's been doing we tell him we left his knapsack on the curb outside the Town Pump.

"Propped against a parking meter," Neil says, "so you'd be sure to see it."

Well, he didn't, Lowell says, and we feel bad about that.

"Was there anything important in it?" Neil asks.

Just a few personal items, Lowell says, a camera and some clothes.

"Hey, maybe it's still there," I say, and although this seems unlikely we go inside the house, call Dallas information, get the number of the Town Pump, and give them a call. It's early afternoon and at first the guy who answers the phone, the day bartender, doesn't want to traipse outside and check the curb for us, but we finally talk him into it. When he comes back, though, he tells us there's nothing out there. He checked every parking meter. No knapsack. How about his lost and found? we say, and he checks that too. Still no knapsack. Obviously it's gone. Somebody took it. Now we feel really bad. Poor Lowell.

He's a thousand miles from home and he doesn't even have a change of underwear. He's going to think we're nothing but a bunch of thieves down here.

"I'm sorry," Neil says. "Can I lend you anything of mine?"

But Lowell just grins. "Listen," he says, "don't worry about it. I never had so much fun in my life. You guys should've been with me. We flew up to this huge ranch near Wichita Falls, a couple of those SMU gals and I. One of them's father owns it. He took me dove hunting two days ago and yesterday he let me pilot his Piper Comanche all the way to Amarillo and back. His daughter's name is Yolanda Rae, and, boy, is she a looker! You guys ever drink triple tequila sunrises at ten thousand feet? I'm not sure but I think I'm engaged!"

"To Yolanda Rae?" Neil says.

"Yeah. I think so. I'm supposed to come back down here for Christmas anyhow, after I talk to my folks."

We're standing in the kitchen at Neil's house. He looks at me and I look back at him. Then Neil, in that way he has, winks and bounces the tennis ball at me. I catch it and, taking my cue as I have so often in the past from him, I wink too and bounce it back to him

"Well, good," Neil says, catching the tennis ball. "I'm glad you had some fun, Lowell. We were beginning to worry about you. We didn't want you leaving here with a bad impression."

## The Retrieval

When I arrived home for the holidays that Christmas of 1954, mother and I weren't getting along. My idea of going off to Paris Junior College to play football had turned out to be a bad one, as she had warned me it would be. Now I was home, and broke, and talking about not going back to PJC in January. Suddenly my life was a mess.

"Well, you can't stay here," mother said when I told her I was through with school. "You can't just lie around the house and expect me to feed you."

Basically, that had been her stance since back in June, following my graduation, at the bottom of my class, from high school. I had spent an aimless summer, loafing, staying out late, sleeping until noon, and then being harangued for it all by mother when I picked her up after work each afternoon in our recently purchased two-tone, black and cream Ford. It was the second car we had ever owned, and easily my favorite. It had an excellent radio, vinyl seat covers, and a roomy back seat for making out in out at the Fox Drive-In Theater. I had quickly come to monopolize the Ford, always seeming to need it just when mother did, and this, too, had become a source of contention between us.

We argued and fought about everything that summer, mother and I. And it went on for weeks. We were tired of each other, sick of each other. There was no talk of me going off to a real college in the fall because there wasn't any money for that. And, besides, with the kind of high school grades I had accumulated, what college would have me? I had been granted a partial scholarship (tuition, room, and books) to play football up at Paris Junior College and had spent my afternoons desultorily "getting in shape" for that over at the high school football field. But then when the time came, and I went off to PJC in late August to begin fall practice, I discovered in quick order that I, one, didn't like the coach, two, didn't like the school (it was smaller, even, than Marshall High School) and, three, didn't like the crummy little town of Paris. So what, I had to ask myself, was I doing there?

Now, home for Christmas, I was having to listen to my own mother tell me she was through feeding me, that, in effect, I was unwanted in my own home. It hurt. I was eighteen years old. She was all I had. I was all *she* had. We had been through a lot together over the years, and suddenly she was signaling that it was time for me to start pulling my own weight. But how? And where? And with what?

Back in November, during the Thanksgiving holidays, my second-best friend Bobby Hughes and I had driven over to Shreveport, Louisiana, to sound out the Marine Corps recruiters there. It had been just a whim. Bobby had gone off to PJC with me to play ball and he was already as sick of the place as I was, but the Marines? That had seemed a bit drastic back then. Still, it hadn't hurt to check them out.

Now, though, it was on the table again. I called Bobby on the telephone—he had already dropped out of PJC weeks before—and asked him if he was ready to go revisit the recruiters. He had been hanging around his own parents' house, underfoot, broke, obnoxious, and was in need of a change of scene himself.

"Sure," he said. "Let's do it. Why not?"

So we went back to Shreveport and, more or less on impulse, signed on the dotted line, committing ourselves to four years of service in the United States Marines. Because the enlistment quota for the Southern Recruitment District had already been filled for the month of January, however, (so the recruiters told us) we would have to wait a month, until February, before the Marine Corps could actually take us to its bosom. So we went back home to Marshall, obligated enlistees now, but sort of on hold until our time came.

Mother took the news calmly. No tears, no expressions of regret for the way things had turned out. "Well, I hope you know what you're doing," was all she said.

Our stature in town, Bobby's and mine, improved overnight, however. When we told people we had joined the Marines and were waiting to be called up, they sort of took a step back mentally and reappraised us. *Maybe these guys will amount to something, after all,* you could see them thinking. Some of the girls we knew were impressed too. We could also see it in their eyes when we told them. *Yeah? The Marines? Won't that be dangerous?*

Interestingly, the one-month waiting period forced on us by our Marine Corps recruiters would have a disastrous impact, as it turned out later, on my educational future. The GI Bill of Rights, which had been revived for the duration of the Korean War, was set to expire on January 31, 1955. I didn't know this, and it wouldn't have meant much to me if I had. All I knew about the GI Bill back then was that it helped you with your mortgage if you were buying a house, and since I wasn't buying a house, so what? That it would also have provided me with roughly one hundred and fifty dollars a month (back when that was real money) during all the time it took me to complete a college degree program of my choosing was totally unknown to me. Nobody had ever told me; I had never thought to ask. But the upshot was that that one-month enlistment delay back in January of 1955 ended up costing me thousands of dollars in future college aid, money I could have dearly used four years later when I finally set out to get myself educated.

At any rate, however, on the morning of February 6, 1955, with tickets provided for us by our Marine recruiters, my friend Bobby Hughes and I boarded a Trailways bus at the Marshall Bus Depot and sat back in our seats for the 150-mile ride to Dallas. We each had on jeans and our Marshall

High School football letter jackets with the big block "M" on the left breast. I was carrying a canvas ditty bag filled with my personal belongings and Bobby had a cardboard suitcase filled with his. In those days all the commercial air traffic for the region flew out of Dallas Love Field, which is where, toward sundown of that same day, Bobby and I boarded a four-engine, propeller-driven American Airlines DC-9, again with tickets provided by our recruiters, for the overnight flight to San Diego, California, and the big Marine Corps Recruit Depot there. With stops in Phoenix and Los Angeles, the flight would take more than ten hours. It was the first time I had ever been in an airplane, of any size, and the thrill of it was enough to keep me awake through most of the night.

Morning found us standing on the tarmac outside the main administration building at MCRD, being yelled at by a pair of Marine sergeants in green fatigues and Smokey-the-Bear hats. We were among a motley assemblage of teenage boys drawn from all over the western half of the country, most of them in jeans, many in letter jackets similar to our own. The sergeants were letting us know, in loud, technicolor fashion, that we weren't civilians anymore. Soon we would be seated half a dozen at a time in chairs at the base barbershop where all the hair would be shorn from our heads in about the time it takes to write this sentence. And so began our thirteen-week introduction to the Marines. "Boot camp," they called it. We were the "boots." Bobby and I got separated almost immediately, he winding up in one recruit platoon and I in another. I would hardly even see him again for the next three months. It was a time of early rising, hurriedly snatched messhall meals, and marching, marching, marching all day long, as slowly the Marine Corps molded us to its own image. I wrote home to mother maybe half a dozen times during this period, telling her what I was up to and how I was doing, and she wrote back to me half a dozen times telling me who she had seen at mass that week and what the weather was like at home.

Gradually my hair grew back in, my marching improved, and I began to stand up considerably straighter. I made friends with boys from Kansas City and Des Moines and Minneapolis, from Little Rock and Tulsa and Moline. There was even a boy from Samoa—*Samoa?*—billeted in the bunk above me, and I made friends with him. As the time of our boot camp graduation approached I found myself in the grip of an *esprit de corps* I would never have imagined myself capable of. I was no longer a civilian indeed. "They" were a loose, lazy, unreliable lot, whereas I was "squared away," "gung ho," a spit-and-polished specimen of military precision and preparedness. I wrote mother one final letter telling her when I would be graduating from boot camp and when, following that, I would be coming home for my first thirty-day leave. I intended to travel by Greyhound.

However, several days after I mailed the letter, I got a long distance phone call. One of my drill instructors summoned me to his office to take the call. It was from mother. She was calling to tell me she had decided to drive out to San Diego, pick me up, and bring me back home for my leave. It would save me bus fare, she explained. *Huh?* I didn't know what to say. The DI was giving me a funny look from behind his desk. *She was coming to get me? Fifteen hundred miles, and she was coming to get me?*

And that's what happened. I graduated from boot camp on a sunny day in May of 1955, and soon after the ceremony there sat mother waiting for me outside the main gate of MCRD in our two-tone, black and cream Ford. She had driven all the way from Marshall in it, all by herself, to bring me back to the nest. Greater love hath no woman.

The boys in my platoon didn't know what to make of it. "She's coming to get you her*self*?" one of them said. "All that way? Boy, she must really like you."

Two of my best buddies in the platoon, Charles ("Chuck") Martin and Kenny Wagner, seized the opportunity to hitch a ride with me heading east. Chuck was from Memphis and Kenny was from St. Louis. They'd be able to save some on

131

their bus fare too. They were both of them well-mannered, fresh-faced boys and mother seemed more than happy to have them along. We left San Diego straightaway in the two-tone Ford, putting MCRD and its harsh regimen rapidly behind us. Mother sat most of the time in the back seat with either Chuck or Kenny beside her. Every time I looked back at her she would smile at me beneficently. She seemed to be enjoying herself immensely. We made good time, stopping only to eat, fill the car up with gas, and go to the restroom. Chuck and Kenny entertained mother with tales of their Tennessee and Missouri upbringings and the car's excellent radio favored us with the popular tunes of the day. Driving straight through, we were able to reach Fort Worth by late afternoon of the second day. Mother's older sister Marie and her family, the Wheelers, lived in Fort Worth, where Uncle Mack Wheeler now worked for Convair, the big airplane manufacturer. The Wheelers seemed to know we were coming, so mother must have said something to them on the way out. Aunt Marie, who was an excellent cook, prepared a quick meal for us of omelettes, toast, and bacon, and Chuck, Kenny and I "chowed down" (as we would have put in back then) on this delicious home-cooked fare, the first we'd had in weeks.

But right about then was when fate, in that slapstick way it sometimes has, intervened. The Wheelers had a teenaged daughter named Anne, and Anne, who was a bit headstrong and quite pretty, had taken an immediate shine to Chuck. Somehow she managed to finagle her way out of the house and into the two-tone Ford, with Chuck at her side, for a little joyride. It all happened very quickly. The rest of us were still at the dinner table. It was evening by then and darkness had descended. The car, with Anne and Chuck in it, hadn't traveled more than three blocks from the Wheelers' house before it collided with a slow-moving freight train at an unmarked railroad crossing. We could hear the sound of the crash—loud, grinding—from the table where we sat.

By some miracle Anne and Chuck escaped with only

bruises, but the car, which was dragged by the train for nearly a block, was a total wreck. Thus ended our brief Fort Worth interlude. Chuck, and Kenny too, seemed somewhat overwhelmed by what had happened. They seemed to be left wondering if these sorts of things—mothers traveling thousands of miles to retrieve their sons, girls appropriating cars and running them headlong into moving trains—were routine occurrences in Texas. They managed to make it onto a couple of Trailways buses the next day to continue their respective journeys to Memphis and St. Louis, but Chuck, and I think Kenny also, left town a bit battered but possibly wiser too.

Mother and I, suddenly without transportation, had to arrange for a replacement car through her insurance agency. And it was in that, not the much loved, so recently annihilated two-tone Ford, that we limped on home to Marshall. I don't remember us having too much to say to each other on the way. I think we were both a little shell-shocked by what had transpired. It was as if it were a metaphor, or something. Still, though, there we were, together again, and headed on home—for what that was worth. I was a spanking-new Marine private, facing four long years of military service that would take me to such places as Camp Pendleton, California; Camp Napunja, Okinawa; the U.S. naval base at Yokosuka, Japan; and, eventually, Twentynine Palms, California; and mother, my dear mother, was a forty-year-old empty nester, her lone chick having finally, somewhat hilariously, flown the coop.

I remember that we stopped for coffee in Mineola on the way home, and that afterwards, when we came back out of the café to the parked replacement car, mother paused, looked at it for a moment,—it was also a Ford, but its color was a pale, listless blue—shook her head and said, "Well, it's okay, I guess. But it's not as, I don't know, *perky* as the other one was, is it?"

# A Gambol on the Golden Shore

### 1.

In the spring of 1954, with high school graduation just weeks away, two other boys and I took it into our heads to drive all the way to California from East Texas to see what we could do about improving the brand of football played out there. There was a junior college in El Centro whose coach, we'd been reliably informed, was aching to get his hands on some genuine Texas athletes. We had no trouble believing this. After all, everyone knew Texas high schools produced the finest football players in the country, didn't they? *Didn't they?*

The distance from Marshall, Texas, to El Centro, California, was roughly fifteen hundred miles, and we figured we could make it in two days driving straight through. So, allowing two days for the return trip and three days for us to check out the place and dazzle those Californians with our gridiron skills, we estimated we'd be gone a week, which would get us back home just in time for the Senior Day Picnic over at Tyler State Park. We didn't want to miss that.

The members of the student body we had shared our plans with were about equally divided in their response. Some thought we were pretty dashing fellows, others thought we were nuts. There was no such division of opinion among the high school faculty and administration, however. They were unanimous in viewing our announced intention as the absolute pinnacle of harebrained irresponsibility.

Nevertheless, we roared out of Marshall on a Wednesday morning in the last week of April, bound for the Golden

State. Behind the wheel was a boy named Marion Morgan. It was his car, a spanking new "sungold" Chevrolet Bel Air convertible, purchased with his mustering out pay from the Army. Marion, having quit school in the tenth grade, had never actually played organized football himself. But he wanted to. It was he who had inflamed us with his reports, over late night porkburgers down at Neely's Brown Pig, of the California coach who was looking for players. A Navy friend of his had put him onto him, he said.

Up front with Marion on that getaway morning was Bobby Hughes, my second-best friend in high school and a 155-pound scatback on our high school team, the Mavericks. Bobby's older sister Dolly, a softie who worked for the telephone company, had loaned him twenty dollars for the trip, which had Bobby feeling fairly well set up.

I was lolling in the backseat with a pile of game jerseys and athletic socks—our wardrobe, along with blue jeans, for the trip—that we'd borrowed from a boy named Vernon Watts, a stockpiler of such apparel, and with three cans of game film we'd talked Coach Charlie Flowers into letting us take along as proof of our prowess. We had also loaded up on Tom's Toasted Peanuts, Moon Pies and Hostess cupcakes, and I had those back there with me too, in a paper sack.

These were the days before the interstate system, when car travel to the West Coast from East Texas was accomplished via U.S. Highway 80, and travelers were obliged to pass through every city and town along the way. By midafternoon of that first day, having successfully made it through sprawling Dallas and congested Fort Worth, we had covered some three hundred miles and only had six hundred more to go to get us out of Texas. Marion's Chevy Bel Air was some car, I had long ago decided. It still had that new car smell and its naugahyde upholstery seemed to me the last word in luxury. Truth to tell, it was probably as much the prospect of riding in this car as it was the idea of playing football out in California that had launched us, Bobby and I anyway, on this cross country trip in the first place.

By midnight I was driving and Marion was asleep in the backseat. We were west of Odessa by then and Bobby and I were whiling away the miles by counting jackrabbits, which had taken to racing across the road in front of our headlights. ("Sixty-seven," Bobby would say, and a few minutes later I'd say, "Sixty-eight.") As dawn broke we were working our way stoplight by stoplight through dusty downtown El Paso. The city was asleep. Not even a service station was open, not even, that we could see, an all-night café. Suddenly, however, a police car emerged out of nowhere and pulled up behind us at a stop light. Two officers got out and approached us with guns drawn. They ordered us out of the car and we did as they said. Marion, who'd been sound asleep, came out of the backseat amid a clatter of empty beer cans, the residue of two six packs we had bought with Marion's fake ID back in Tarrant County. The policemen spread-eagled us over the hood of the Chevy, patted us down, then ordered us to follow them to the station two blocks away. There, we were booked, had our belts and shoelaces taken away, and were marched upstairs to a large metal holding cell—all of this taking place in seemingly no time at all. One minute we were winging our way to California and the next we were sitting in a big iron cage in the El Paso jail.

I was mortified. What was my widowed mother going to think? She hadn't wanted me to make this fool trip in the first place; she'd tried to talk me out of it. But I was seventeen and a football hero and had long since quit listening to her. Why were we in the El Paso jail? Well, it seems there had been a burglary back in Marshall. It happened shortly before we left town. Someone broke into Vernon Watts's bedroom and stole his collection of silver dollars, coins he had been saving to buy an engagement ring for his girlfriend, Marsha Nell. This was the same Vernon Watts from whom we'd borrowed the jerseys and athletic socks we were now wearing, but he knew about that and had said we could. And, okay, there hadn't been anybody home at his house when we went out there, but we hadn't stolen his damn money. At least I didn't think we had. I looked at Bobby. He looked at me. We both looked at Marion. Everyone protested his innocence.

Meanwhile, though, there we sat in the El Paso jail. Minutes passed, an hour. The cell had another occupant besides us. He was a Mexican-appearing fellow in his mid-twenties, goodlooking in a Mexican sort of way. He watched us and grinned, giving me the impression he had been there, in jail, before. After a while he moved to the front of the cell and began a conversation, through a gap in the metal flooring, with some women in a cell directly below us. The talk was in Spanish. There was an amount of bantering back and forth, incomprehensible to us, then he broke out a long piece of string which he proceeded to dangle through the gap, down to the other cell. A moment later he brought it carefully back up and, lo and behold, there was a sandwich attached to the other end! As he sat there eating it he watched us watching him. He grinned again. *"Tiene hambre?"* he said, and when we just stared blankly at him, "Joo hongry?" We admitted we were, and before long the Mexican was fishing below for sandwiches for us all. They were just baloney on white bread but they tasted pretty good after all the peanuts and cupcakes we'd been subsisting on.

It was Marion who asked our benefactor who the women below us were. *"Putas,"* he said. "Whores." Our interest, already avid, quickened. "Do you know any of them?" Bobby asked, and the Mexican said he knew all of them, they were his friends.

"Can you fix us up with them?"

"Joo got money?" the Mexican said.

"Some," Bobby said, turning cagey.

"Let me see," the Mexican said.

Bobby reached for his wallet and, finding nothing back

there, forced us to recall that these too had been confiscated, along with our belts and shoelaces. "Rats," Bobby said. "The cops took it."

The Mexican grinned. "Too bad," he said. "*Pobrecito.*"

Our whorish fantasies evaporated in the face of this renewed realization of where we were, what we were doing there, and soon a sort of silent funk had settled over our jail cell. Another hour passed. Then another. What was going on? Were they planning to keep us there indefinitely? I began having visions of myself as a convict, a jailbird. No more football. No more Dairy Queen sundaes. No more Sue Ellen Grimes in the back seat of mother's car at the Fox Drive-in.

By mid-afternoon the gloom was thick where we were. The Mexican had retreated to his own corner of the cell and was playing solitaire with a deck of cards he'd produced from somewhere. The rest of us had long since run out of things to say to each other. Bobby tried to sleep. Marion had a shoe and sock off and was picking at his toenails. I sat with my arms folded, trying to keep my mind from racing. No more Sue Ellen Grimes!

Suddenly, all unannounced, someone was standing at the cell door. It was our jailer. He unlocked the door with his big key and motioned us out. "Okay," he said. "Let's go."

He didn't have to ask us twice. We scrambled up off the hard metal deck and hurried out after him. Marion didn't even bother to put his sock and shoe back on, just carried them in his hand.

"*Adios, muchachos,*" the Mexican said, looking up from his card game.

Downstairs, we were given back our belts and shoelaces, along with the rest of our belongings, and told we were free to go. No one explained why. It was the best news I had had in my entire life. I moved about the room shaking hands with anyone who would shake hands with me. "Thank you," I said. "Thank you, thank you." And moments later we were standing back outside in the hot El

Paso sunlight, three happy youngsters, grateful to be free.

By the time we reached Las Cruces, New Mexico, however, less than an hour away, our brief stopover in the El Paso pokey had been transformed into a real-life adventure, starring us. Bobby was remembering how big the Mexican's eyes got when he, Bobby, reached for his wallet. "I think he thought I had a knife," Bobby said. And that's when Marion, our elder, giving us the benefit of his experience, brought up the possibility of the Mexican having been a stool pigeon, placed in the cell to extract information from us to be passed on to the authorities. "They do that, you know," he said, "especially in the tougher lockups, and the El Paso jail's supposed to be one of the toughest in the country." *One of the toughest in the country.* We thought about that. One of the toughest in the country and we had been there—but now we were out, loose, at large. We milked this, massaged it, for a while longer, then, changing the subject, Marion said, "Goddamn that Vernon Watts. He's cost us half a day's travel. We ought to stomp his butt when we get home. Y'all agree?" We did indeed, and we continued on in this vein for a while: treacherous Vernon Watts and the retribution that awaited him when we got home for having messed with three veterans of the El Paso jail.

By nightfall, though, we were back to counting jackrabbits. *A hundred and forty-seven... a hundred and forty-eight...a hundred and forty-nine...* If we'd thought West Texas was empty, that was before we tried crossing New Mexico and Arizona, where it was sixty miles between towns and the towns—Lordsburg, Deming, Willcox, Benson—were nothing but gas stations with a trading post anyway, and the only radio stations we could pick up were either gospel or Spanish-language. *A hundred and sixty-three...a hundred and sixty-four...a hundred and sixty-five...*

At dawn, however, we were approaching the California border, with our destination less than a hundred miles away, and the excitement inside the Chevy was palpable. We'd made it. Our long trip was almost over, an accomplishment in itself. They knew we were coming too, were expecting us. Marion's friend, the Navy man, had talked by telephone with the coach and we had the coach's address for when we got to town. Now it was just a matter of chewing up these remaining few miles in this excellent car and then wallowing in all the attention we knew awaited us.

Marion was asleep in back again. Bobby was driving, and he and I had been discussing what kind of scholarship we expected these people to offer us. As Texas high school footballers we were connoisseurs of the various types of college athletic scholarships available. It was something we had been talking about since the ninth grade.

"Well, you can do what you want to," Bobby said finally, "but me, I'm looking for a full ride. I wouldn't feel right settling for anything else."

The "full ride" was the holy grail of athletic scholarships, the gold standard. It consisted of room, board, tuition, and books, plus a negotiated amount of "laundry money" that was said to vary greatly from school to school, with the big Southwest Conference schools like Texas, SMU, and Baylor offering the most.

"How about laundry money?" I said. "What do you think's fair?"

"Thirty a week?" Bobby said. "I think I could get by on thirty a week. How about you?"

I mulled this over, giving careful consideration to what it was we were prepared to do for these people, the glory we were prepared to bring them. "I don't know," I said. "Thirty sounds a little low to me."

"Forty?" Bobby said.

"That sounds more like it."

"Okay, forty it is then," Bobby said. "Let's make a pact. We don't settle for anything less than a full ride and forty a week."

We shook on it, right there in the front seat of Marion Morgan's 1954 Chevy Bel Air, doing sixty miles an hour on

U.S. Highway 80. We would play football for El Centro Junior College, but we wouldn't sell ourselves cheaply. We owed it to ourselves not to. We owed it to Texas.

## 2.

"Welcome to California," the big sign just beyond Yuma had said about an hour ago, and now, almost before we knew it, we were approaching the outskirts of El Centro. It was not as I had pictured it. Although you could see on a map that it was inland, not one of the fabled coastal cities such as San Diego or San Francisco, still, this was California, land of glamour and enchantment, home of movie stars, hot rods, and surfers, and one had certain mental images. All of which El Centro fell considerably short of. It was just another dusty little Western town. Agriculture, it turned out, was the main activity around there, thereby accounting for all the irrigation ditches we'd been passing lately. The commercial architecture was a bit more Spanish-looking than you might find in East Texas, but otherwise it looked not unlike Marshall, and it was about the same size.

The address we'd been given turned out to be right downtown, at a corner of the main intersection. The man we were looking for, the coach, was named Bud Hollis, but the building occupying the spot where we expected to find him was a commercial, not a residential, one, with street-level shops, closed at that hour, under an arcade. There was an exposed stairway mid-building, though, and after some hesitation we took this up to the second floor where we confronted, of all things, a large open-air swimming pool. A sign announced that we'd arrived at the "Civic Natatorium." I had no idea what that meant. A fellow in gym shorts and a tank top was raking the pool with the help of a long pole, however, and we approached him and asked if he knew where we could find Bud Hollis.

*He* was Bud Hollis! Turned out he managed the

swimming pool in the off-season as a way to supplement his income from coaching out at the junior college. He and his wife and two small children had an apartment up there overlooking the pool. He seemed like a thoroughly nice man, very open, very genial, and, best of all, glad to see us. He *had* been contacted by the Navy man, knew we were coming, and had sort of expected us last night. We apologized for the delay but didn't go into what had caused it.

"Have you had breakfast?" he said, and soon we were seated at the dining table up in the apartment as Coach Hollis's pretty wife scurried about preparing scrambled eggs and sausages for us. The Hollis's young son was there too, being fed before going off to school, and at one point he looked up at me and said, "Are you gonna play football for my dad?"

I smiled at the lad, and in my most magnanimous fashion allowed that, "We might."

This brought smiles all around the table and we sat there eating and chatting, warmed by the glow of possibility. Coach Hollis asked us a number of questions about the high school football program back home; he seemed especially interested in the game films we told him we had brought. Apparently the idea of filming one's games for instructional purposes was a technological breakthrough that hadn't yet reached California—which might have seemed ironic to us if we had thought about it, California being home to the nation's movie industry and all. "After you've eaten," the coach said, "I'll take you over to the campus and show you around. There's a photographer coming at ten, or whenever I call him, and I've got a couple of our current players I want you to meet that'll be joining us too. Maybe we can all sit down and look at those films together this afternoon."

A *photographer?* They were going to take our *picture?* This was beginning to sound like the Big Time. "What kind of photographer?" Bobby asked.

"Fella from the paper," the coach said. "He knows you're coming."

"The *news*paper?"

"Yep."

Bobby and I looked at each other. We were grinning ear to ear. Marion seemed slightly less thrilled, and I got the impression he had never had his picture appear much of anywhere before, except maybe in the "Our Boys in the Service" section of the paper back home. But Bobby and I knew the value of publicity for athletes. Having your picture in the paper the day after a game, especially if it was an action shot, was how you created an image for yourself. We knew this because we had been looking at such pictures of others—Doak Walker, Kyle Rote, Bobby Layne—since before we were old enough to read.

And, sure enough, a couple of hours later there we were out at El Centro Junior College, standing under the goalposts at the football field, having our picture snapped by a photographer from the local newspaper. And not only that, we were having it taken in full football uniform (except for the shoes): the red and black silks of the El Centro Red Devils, which Coach Hollis had had us change into over in the locker room. The picture, a two-column shot of the three of us, from the knees up, would appear in the paper the next day above a caption identifying us as "Texas Athletes Here to Help ECJC."

After the picture-taking session we changed back into our street clothes—jeans and jerseys—and the coach took us over to his "office" in the school gym. It was really just a desk and some chairs in one of the equipment rooms, and we sat there for a while among the medicine balls and tumbling mats waiting for the two current ECJC players, who were to be our hosts for the weekend, we'd learned, to show up, which eventually they did.

Their names were Billy Pyle and Kay Hargrove and they were impressive physical specimens. They seemed much older than we were, more physically mature, and I was suddenly embarrassed for Marion, in particular, who, though himself older than Bobby and I, had just recently cut a very poor figure in his ECJC football uniform. Bobby and I had had to help him with his shoulder pads, for one thing; he'd tried to put them on backwards. And then when we did get him properly suited up, his painfully thin legs had been a sight to see. I couldn't help wondering what Coach Hollis must think. In uniform, Marion simply did not look like a football player.

But even in street clothes, Billy Pyle and Kay Hargrove most emphatically did. Big, wide-shouldered, well-muscled, they carried themselves with the looseness and grace that good athletes have. Billy had been a halfback on the past year's team, we learned, and Kay, who was somewhat stockier, had been the fullback. Coach Hollis introduced us to them and they seemed genuinely pleased to make our acquaintance. It was something I was already beginning to notice about Californians: their openness, their friendliness, their air of awareness that they were fortunate to be living where they did—instead of wherever it was you lived—and their belief that there was more than enough of whatever it was they thought they had to go around.

After the introductions, Coach Hollis took us all over to the school cafeteria and fed us ("This one's on ECJC"), and then we all trooped back to the equipment room where it was time to view those game films. Pyle and Hargrove seemed as excited at the prospect as Coach Hollis had been. A projector was set up, and a screen, and soon we were all watching the flickering, black-and-white recreation of last year's game with the Lufkin High School Panthers. The film had been shot with a single camera perched atop the press box at Maverick Stadium and all the action appeared to be taking place about a quarter of a mile away. There was no such thing as a close-up.

"That's me going off tackle there," I had to say. "Number thirty-one." Or, "Here's Bobby on an end sweep—number twenty-two." And, "Here's where Eubanks drops the pass that costs us the district championship. He catches that and it's on to bi-district." On and on I went like this, and the Californians couldn't seem to get enough of it. They were leaning forward in their chairs, the coach too, like nine-year-olds at a matinee western. They kept backing the film up to show plays over again. We ended up spending the whole afternoon there in the equipment room watching those jittery, slightly out of focus high school game films. When we finally emerged from the place our stock appeared to have gone up considerably, and, across the way, the sun was dropping low behind the football stadium.

It was Friday evening, and we were on our own. A beach party and a cookout had been planned for us for Saturday night, we'd learned, and we were supposed to meet back with the coach on Sunday morning to talk business. But Friday had been left open because no one knew for sure when we were coming. Coach Hollis had put us up in a guest dorm there on the ECJC campus. It was just a bare room with two double-decker bunks, but that was fine with us. It was better than sleeping in the car. But what to do with our Friday night free time?

Well, El Centro, it turned out, was only fifteen miles from the Mexican border. This was news to us. We didn't even know California *had* a Mexican border. Was Baja California part of Mexico? You could have fooled us. As soon as night fell, however, we set out for Mexicali, Baja California, Republic of Mexico, which turned out to be a fairly typical border settlement. There was a cantina called "El Oso Negro" in the center of town and we made our way straight for it. Except for us, the place was nearly empty, even though it was Friday night. There were a couple of middle-aged rancher types over at one table and some dowdy looking Mexican women at another one, but that was about it. As far as paying customers went, we seemed to be the main action, and that was fine with us. Little barefoot kids kept coming through, though, distracting us, cutting into our party time. They tried to sell us chewing gum. They tried to sell us flowers. They tried to sell us picture postcards. Finally, Bobby bought a pair of sunglasses from one of them for a dollar and proceeded to put them on and wear them there in the darkness of the cantina. Marion, not to be outdone, bought a deck of cards with naked ladies on them.

After a while some younger women and girls came in and sat down at a table nearby. There were five of them. The oldest looked to be in her mid-twenties and the youngest no older than Bobby or me. They all had on shiny, sateen dresses and high heels and lots of makeup. In the bad light of the cantina they looked pretty good, especially a couple of the younger ones. They smiled in our direction and one of them waved at us.

"Hey, did you see that?" Bobby said. "She waved at me."

"I think she likes you," Marion said. "Go over there and talk to her."

"It's those shades," I said. "She thinks you're Tab Hunter."

The girl was still waving at us. A couple of the others were now waving too. There were also lots of smiles emanating from the other table. Then, from out of nowhere—just like those El Paso policemen—a young man materialized. Suddenly he was at our table, bending over us. He couldn't have been much older than we were. "You like these girls?" he was saying. "You want to get to know them?" We looked up at him. Where had he come from? He continued speaking to us, rapidly, smoothly. He looked Mexican, but his English was better than ours. He knew these girls personally, he said. He had gone to school with them. They were very clean, very passionate. They knew what a man liked. Five dollars would buy a whole night with one of them, three dollars would buy a shorter time. He gazed into our rapt, upturned faces. "Anyone interested?" he said.

Later, on the drive back to El Centro, we compared

notes. Bobby's girl was named Maria Elena, he said, and had a brother in Lubbock who worked in a car wash. Mine was named Concepta, I told them, and was earning money to go to cosmetology school. ("Lice on or lice off?" she'd asked, puzzling me until I realized she was saying "lights.") Marion said he hadn't bothered to get his girl's name, but if he ever went back there he was going to ask for her again because she was a true professional. How so? we wondered. What did she do? "Everything," Marion said. "You name it." We tried (naming it), but soon ran out of possibilities. Marion, acting smug, and older, refused to be more explicit, though we pressed him for some time.

Mid-morning of the next day we were sleeping soundly in the bare dorm room when a  car pulled up outside and Billy Pyle and Kay Hargrove came bounding in.  It was time to head  up to Brawley, they said, where arrangements were already underway for that evening's beach party and cookout. Hargrove had a copy of the local newspaper with him and he plopped it down in front of us. There at the top of the second—"Valley Views"—section was the picture ("Texas Athletes Here to Help ECJC") that had been taken the day before, with me squinting at the camera, Bobby, his chin thrust out, looking militant, and Marion, his thin neck rising from the deep well of his shoulder pads, looking the complete impostor, God love him, that he was.

Brawley, it turned out, was a slightly larger town some fifteen miles north of El Centro.  It billed itself as the hub city of the Imperial Valley, which the signs told us contained some of the richest farmland on earth.  "We Feed the Nation," the signs bragged. And indeed Brawley did seem a step up from El Centro: cleaner, more prosperous-looking, more *Californian*. There were palm trees lining the streets, for instance, and lots of fine "ranch-style" houses with wide, manicured lawns. Everybody, even the kids, seemed to be driving a brand new car.  Brightly painted hotrods abounded, making Marion's sungold Chevy look almost dowdy by comparison. *This*, I started to feel, was it. This was what we'd come for.

"Let's go find Drollinger," Kay Hargrove said. "See what's happening." He was in Marion's car with us, giving directions. Pyle was following in the other vehicle. We set off in search of "Drollinger," who, surprisingly, turned out to be a girl, first name: Pam. And she was gorgeous. I'd never in my life seen anyone so pretty. There wasn't a girl in all East Texas that pretty. She came out to the curb to greet us, when we pulled up in front of her parents' house, wearing shorts and a wrinkled t-shirt. Her figure was remarkable, as was her tan. Now this, indisputably, I thought, was California. She and Hargrove chatted for a moment at curb side, then he asked her if she was going to be able to "shake loose" and join us. She said she was "leaning" but she needed to talk to another girl first. "You guys in a sweat?" she said. "You wanta come hang while I buzz her?' Hargrove said we had to "split" but she should give her friend a ring, though, and the two of them could come out together.

I was sitting in the backseat with Bobby, absorbing all this California dialog, trying to get used to girls being called by their last names, to everyone, whether male or female, being referred to as "guys." Billy Pyle had gotten out of the other car by now and come up beside Drollinger. He draped an arm over her shoulder familiarly. "Be on your best behavior, Drollinger," he said. "These guys are here to save us."

Drollinger looked in and bathed us with her smile; it was like headlights being turned on. "Oh, I hope so," she said.

A short time later we were driving through the countryside, on our way to a reservoir outside Brawley. It was a mild spring afternoon with warm breezes rustling in the tall palms overhead. Water gushed in the irrigation ditches on either side of the road, and out in the fields we passed were crops of spinach, cantaloupe, and asparagus.

At the reservoir there was a fine sandy beach, and by late afternoon we had the portable grills set up, had the charcoal going, had the chests of iced-down beer firmly planted in the shade of some ocotillo shrubs, had some easy listening California tunes coming from someone's portable radio ("*Hey there, you with the stars in your eyes…*") and were well launched toward an evening of outdoor fun.

The reservoir reminded me of the lake at Tyler State Park back home. It was about the same size, at any rate, and the water temperature, surprisingly, was about the same. There were maybe twenty of us partiers, all told, at least half of whom were girls. Pyle and Hargrove had supplied swimming suits for Bobby, Marion and me—we not having thought to bring our own, of course—and in between bouts of beer drinking and tossing one of the several footballs around on the sand, we took an occasional dip in the somewhat chilly water. All the Californians were big swimmers, I saw, males and females alike. They seemed much more at home in the water than we were. There was lots of splashing, head-dunking, and other horseplay on their part, girls included, as we, meanwhile, more or less squatted in the shallows and watched.

It was also impossible not to notice that the Californians were, without exception, better physical specimens than we were. Their teeth were straighter and whiter, their complexions clearer, their postures better. Most of the boys were members of the ECJC football team, and as such were maybe a year or two older than Bobby and me, but they seemed much bigger, better muscled, more physically mature. As for the girls, they were uniformly pretty. Lithe, tanned, and self-confident, they bounded about the beach as if they were born to it. There were two or three bikinis in the group, though none of the extreme variety—this *was* 1954, after all—and Bobby, Marion and I had trouble keeping our eyes in our heads at times. The California males, of course, didn't even seem to notice that some of these girls were nearly naked. For all they cared, they might have been wearing nun's habits.

By nightfall, with the coals dying in the grills and several pounds of hot dogs and hamburgers digesting in our stomachs, we were nestled on the still-warm sand in small groups, having paired off, most of us, with someone of the other sex. Lucky me, I was with Drollinger and I was telling her all about myself: what TV shows I liked, what my favorite movies and popular songs were, and so on. She couldn't believe I watched Arthur Godfrey. I didn't tell her we only got one TV channel in Marshall, out of Shreveport, Louisiana, and that Godfrey was mostly what was on it. She asked me what I thought of him firing singer Julius LaRosa, and I said I thought LaRosa had it coming. Then she asked me what my favorite color was, and I said green.

"Why green?" she said.

"I don't know—because it matches my eyes?"

"Your eyes aren't green."

"Yeah, they are." (No, they weren't.)

"Let me see."

It was fairly dark by then, and there was no way she could tell what color my eyes were, but she bent down over me anyway, pretending to examine them. And right at that moment we heard a voice from out front of us, just a few feet away.

"Drollinger? You dumb bitch, where are you?"

It was Kay Hargrove. He'd been drinking beer all afternoon, more of it, even, than the rest of us, and he had been acting belligerent for the past couple of hours: throwing the football too hard from too close up, dunking people with a bit too much enthusiasm, and so on. Now he was standing out there in front of Pam Drollinger and me with his fists on his hips and his legs spread apart in the sand.

"Kay," she answered him. "What is it? I'm right here."

What was she doing down there? he wanted to know. Talking, she told him. "We're discussing the firing of Julius

LaRosa. Why?"

"I've been looking for you."

"Well, now you've found me."

"Yeah, now I've found you."

Silence. Drollinger didn't say anything. Hargrove, fists still on hips, stood there glaring down at us.

"Hey, there, Kay," I said. "What's up?"

"Keep outta this, Dogpatch," he said. "I'm talking to her."

He began to berate the girl, loudly, drunkenly, and she continued to do her best to placate him. Whenever I tried to intercede, he would turn on me, fiercely, calling me "Hayseed" and "Dogpatch" and, for some reason, deriding the game films he had been so avid about the day before. At one point he said, "You Texas Okies think you're hot stuff, don't you?" Hargrove was bigger than I was, and, as I've indicated, better muscled; I wasn't eager to tangle with him. Drollinger put a hand on my arm as if to restrain me, but she needn't have bothered. I wasn't going anywhere. Hargrove kept up his harangue until finally, with a sigh, she got up and began to gather her things. "I'd better go talk to him," she said. "He's had a little too much to drink."

She went off with Hargrove and I sat there on the sand waiting for her to come back, but she never did. Eventually the party began to dissolve, people packing up and heading for their cars. Bobby and Marion had joined me and some of the ECJC team members stopped by as they were leaving to tell us it was nice meeting us and they hoped to see us in the fall. One of them told me not to worry about Hargrove, he was a good guy, he just got a little mean sometimes when he'd been drinking. On the way back to El Centro, Bobby— it was just we three Texans in Marion's car now—asked me what Hargrove had been so upset about. I said it seemed to be our game films, of all things.

"Well, screw him then," Bobby said. "Just because they never thought to film their own damn games—what kind of rinky-dink operation are they running out here anyway?"

It was something I had begun to wonder about myself. I'd been struck by how small the stadium was the day before, no bigger than our high school one back home, and by how tiny and cramped the press box was. I mentioned this to Bobby. He suggested we bring it up with Coach Hollis the next day. "You still holding out for a full ride?" I said. Bobby said he was. I said so was I. We asked Marion and he said he wouldn't take anything less than we got.

It was a pact, then; we all clasped hands. "Full rides or nothing."

Coach Hollis's wife had prepared a huge breakfast for us. There were omelettes and bacon, and waffles if we wanted them. There were sweet rolls and biscuits and several kinds of jam. There was even something called guava juice, which was supposed to be high in fiber and muscle-building protein. It was our last day in California. We showed up at the swimming-pool apartment on time but looking a little the worse for wear. Having opted at the last minute the evening before for one more quick run to Mexicali (Concepta said she was "soo-priced" to see me again so soon), we hadn't got back to the guest dorm until near dawn.

"Dig in, fellas," Coach Hollis said when we were seated at the table. "Don't let it get cold."

Billy Pyle had joined us, but Kay Hargrove wasn't there. The coach said he had something else to do and might show up later. Pyle whispered that he had a monster hangover.

"How was the cookout?" the coach said. "Did they show you a good time? Bill, did Ramirez and the others show up?" Pyle assured him there was a good turnout for the party, lots of people showed up. Nobody mentioned Kay Hargrove's antics.

Marion said, "Pass the biscuits."

Bobby said, "I'll have one of those waffles."

I said, "Guava juice, huh? Not bad. Not bad."

Sometime later, after the dishes were cleared, Coach Hollis

suggested we all go down and sit at one of the poolside tables. "Bill," he said to Pyle, "Why don't you stay up here and help Marge with the dishes?" The three of us followed Coach Hollis out of the apartment and down to the pool, where we sat down with him around one of the metal tables there. It was clear from the coach's expression that the time had come to talk turkey. I put on my game face and so did Bobby. Marion just sat.

"Well, fellas," the coach said with no preamble, "what do you think? Have you seen enough? Would you like to come out here and play for us? If you would, we'd love to have you. I think you'd like it around here. It's a good area. The people are steady and God-fearing. The school's fairly new but I think you can get a pretty good education here, depending on what you want to study. We're big in crop management, soil science, and the like. Have you had a chance to talk it over among yourselves yet?"

Bobby and I looked at each other. Marion looked at both of us. We couldn't decide who ought to speak.

"Um," I began, "what's the deal? What do we get if we do decide to come here? Besides the education, I mean."

The coach looked at each of us in turn. He had a puzzled expression on his face. "What do you mean 'get'?"

"What kind of scholarships are you offering?" Bobby said.

"Scholarships?"

"Yeah, you know. Room, board, tuition—stuff like that. What kind of deal would you give us?" I said.

"Laundry money," Bobby said, nudging me. "Don't forget the laundry money."

The coach appeared perplexed. "Wait a second, fellas," he said. "Hold on. There must be some—"

"We was thinking along the lines of a full ride," Marion said, his face showing his pride at having mastered the term.

"Plus laundry money," Bobby insisted. "I myself, personally, would need at least forty a week in laundry money. I can't speak for these other two, but that's what I'd need. Forty. Minimum."

"Me too," Marion chimed in. "I ain't taking anything less than he gets."

The coach was shaking his head. "Fellas," he was saying. "Fellas. Whoa. Let's come back down to earth here. There's obviously been a mistake of some kind. We don't offer scholarships at ECJC. We're a *junior* college. The state doesn't allow it. We can maybe help you with a part-time job, setting siphon hoses out in the onion fields, working in a packing plant or something. We help some of the boys that way. But no scholarships. That's just not a possibility."

We were stunned. Were we hearing the man correctly?

"Not even room and board?" I said.

"Not even tuition and books?" said Bobby.

The coach just shook his head.

Silence fell over the poolside table. Could it be that we had driven fifteen hundred miles and jeopardized our (or at least Bobby's and my) high school graduation for a mirage? A chimera? For something that didn't even exist? The fact was just too awful to contemplate. We'd be laughingstocks back home. We'd never hear the end of it. What would we tell people? What could we possibly say?

I turned to Marion. "I thought you said your Navy buddy said—"

Marion showed us his palms. "Hell," he said. "He *did*. He said they were looking for players and they'd give us anything we wanted. That's exactly what he told me. I swear to God."

We looked at the coach.

"What Navy buddy?" he said. "Did he go to school here?"

We looked back at Marion.

"I *think* so," Marion said.

"Is he the fella who called me and said you were coming out?"

"Yeah," Marion said, relieved to have the Navy buddy's existence, at least, confirmed. "That's him."

"All he said was that you were coming. He said you played high school ball in Texas and were looking for somewhere to continue playing. There wasn't any talk of scholarships or anything like that."

We looked at Marion, Bobby and I. Marion just sat there, showing us his palms.

Silence descended again on the little poolside table. I looked down into the pale, greenish water just a few feet from where we sat. Overnight, a few eucalyptus leaves had blown into it from somewhere and were floating now on the pool's surface. The coach was going to have to get his rake out again.

Finally, after what seemed like a long time, Marion said, "Those part-time jobs—how much would they pay?"

3.

"A hundred and ninety-two," Bobby said. Then, "A hundred and ninety-three."

We were back on Highway 80, heading east through Arizona at sundown, counting jackrabbits. The mood in the sungold Chevy was not good. Marion sat hunched over the wheel with Bobby in the seat beside him. I was in the back with the cans of game film that were supposed to make all the difference, but hadn't. I was considering throwing them out the window. Marion had quit being defensive by now and gone on the attack. "It was y'alls' idea as much as it was mine," he said. Going to California, he meant. "And don't try to deny it." Bobby said he wasn't denying anything; he just wished Marion had asked his Navy buddy a few more questions—like, for example, *did they offer fucking scholarships out there?* Marion said, what did he know about scholarships? He hadn't even finished the tenth grade. Bobby said he acted like he knew. Marion said, no, he didn't. Bobby said, yes, he did.

"A hundred and ninety-eight," I said.

By the time we reached the New Mexico border I had begun to realize I was never going to see Concepta again.

Suddenly I missed her. Already. Then I realized I didn't even know her last name. "Hey," I said to Bobby, "if you were gonna write a letter to someone in Mexico, how would you go about it? Just address it to such and such and so and so in Mexicali, Mexico?"

"Yeah," Bobby said. "Stick a stamp on it."

"How big a stamp?"

"I don't know. Ask the post office."

"Could you just send it to someone's first name, in care of a bar, do you think?"

"You could *try*. I don't know what the Mexican mail service is like, but if it's like everything else down there, I wouldn't hold my breath 'til she gets it."

It was a depressing thought: having to rely on the Mexican postal authorities to see that a teenaged prostitute, whose last name you didn't even know, got a letter from you addressed in care of a bar. Might as well put it in a bottle and drop it in the Rio Grande, hope it could float upstream.

"Shit," I said.

"Two hundred and thirty-six," said Bobby.

Retracing our route was not nearly as much fun as laying it down in the first place. What had seemed adventurous and exciting before became stale and commonplace the second time around. When we reached El Paso, scene of our earlier, now mythic (in our minds) police encounter, we had no desire to linger. With the jackrabbit count approaching three hundred and our little corner of East Texas still nine hundred miles away, all we wanted to do was keep going. "Wonder if that ol' boy is still fishing for baloney sandwiches up there in jail?" was all anyone said.

Outside of Pecos, in a rainstorm, something not a jackrabbit crossed the highway in front of our headlights. It was large and black and moving very fast, with a long, loping gait. "Hey," I said, "did you see that?"

I was driving now, with Bobby in the front seat beside me. Marion was snoring in back. It was sometime after midnight. "Yeah," Bobby said. "What was it?"

I said I didn't know, but it wasn't a jackrabbit.

"A cat maybe?" Bobby said.

It was too big for a cat, I said.

"I mean, like, you know—a panther?"

I looked at Bobby. A panther. I wasn't aware that they had panthers in West Texas, not black ones anyway, but it was an intriguing notion. "A panther," I said, playing with the idea. "You really think so?"

"I don't know," Bobby said, "but if it wasn't, it's the biggest damn house cat I ever saw."

I drove on in silence, pondering what we'd just witnessed. It did nothing to lighten my mood. Or Bobby's either, I could tell. A big black cat had crossed our path. Around midnight. Given all we'd been through, it seemed eerily fitting.

Daylight found us re-entering the known world. By mid-morning we were on the outskirts of Fort Worth ("Where the West Begins") and could begin to think thoughts of East Texas and home. Bobby was driving and I was slumped against the passenger-side window, fighting sleep. Marion was sitting up in the backseat by now, but looking gray-faced like the rest of us and just as out of sorts. We were all three exhausted: physically, emotionally, spiritually. Three thousand miles of straight-through driving in a little over six days will take it out of you, even at seventeen.

We'd been discussing what to do, head straight on home to Marshall or swing by Tyler State Park as we'd originally planned? The consensus seemed to be to skip Tyler, limp home, try to forget the whole sorry business. If we went to Tyler, what would we say? There were bound to be a lot of questions.

We made it through Fort Worth and then Dallas in stony silence. This had been an endurance test and we were still in danger of failing it. But we were in the home stretch now, and as we passed through Forney and Terrell and began to get our first whiffs of East Texas, we rallied a little. Soon Wills Point would be coming up and with it the beginning of the piney woods. We'd have come in off the plains.

We were still on Highway 80, as we had been so much of the time, both going and coming, for days. At Mineola, however, suddenly there was a sign that said Tyler was only twenty miles away, on Highway 69, if we chose to take the turn-off, which was coming up fast. We were 75 miles from Marshall. We had to decide. We took the turn-off. And within twenty minutes we were pulling into Visitors' Parking at Tyler State Park, where sat, bold as you please, three big yellow-and-black school buses from the Harrison County Independent School District. That was us! Like a stray come home to the litter we parked Marion's Chevy right up alongside them. We didn't bother to change socks and jerseys or spruce up in any way, simply headed straight down for the beach.

The first of our classmates to see us coming got these frozen, astonished looks on their faces. *Who were these guys?* It was if they recognized us, but then again they didn't. Somehow we had been transformed. We were Meriwether Lewis and William Clark. We were Ferdinand Magellen, Ernest Shackleton, Christopher Columbus—*Marco Polo!*—returned with news of other, grander worlds.

They crowded around us. They wanted to hear, *needed* to. We described for them the wonders of what we'd seen: the riches of Cathay, the Hanging Gardens of Babylon, moonlight on the Ganges, Antarctica's frigid and trackless wastes, Tahiti with its dark and dusky maidens, Kilimanjaro and its snow-capped peak…

Someone said they'd heard we were in jail. And, yes, we told them, it was true. Devil's Island, the Chateau d'If, Dannemora with its cold, hard walls, the pitiless cliffs of Sing-Sing… None of these were alien to us now.

And, more, they insisted, tell us more. So we did. Safe on the domesticated sands of Tyler State Park, back among the familiar pines and hackberry bushes of East Texas, we rambled on and on about forbidden pleasures and riotous nights, about this and that and such and so and a thousand other things.

The silly, inconsequential business of the football scholarships never even came up.

.

## Coda: Roy vs. Gene

When I was a little boy growing up in Texas during the 1940's, we male youngsters divided ourselves into two distinct camps. There was the Roy Rogers camp and the Gene Autry camp. I belonged to the latter.

Gene had won my allegiance for any number of good reasons. He was from Tioga, Texas, for one thing, whereas Rogers was from somewhere up in Ohio. Ohio? Who ever heard of a cowboy, even a singing one, from Ohio? And, besides, Roy Rogers wasn't even his real name. His real name, if you could believe it, was Leonard Slye. Leonard Slye? Who ever heard of a cowboy named Leonard Slye?

Being an Autry partisan meant that, naturally, I also favored Gene's horse, Champion, over Roy's horse, Trigger. Both were noble animals, I might admit if forced to, but Champion was faster. How did I know this? Well, I didn't. Some things you just have to take on faith. When they galloped across the screen during one of those obligatory chase scenes, though, it did seem to me that Champion's ears lay back flatter against his skull than Trigger's did. Not conclusive evidence of greater speed, maybe, but a strong indicator. And, anyhow, Champion, with that white blaze on his forehead, was prettier than Trigger, whose tawny, effete palomino-ness didn't photograph nearly as well up there on the big black-and-white screen.

When it came to sidekicks, I thought Smiley Burnett had it all over the grubby-looking Gabby Hays. No contest there. Smiley's white horse sported that black (painted) ring around its eye, which I thought was cute and funny, as was the way Smiley wore his cowboy hat, its brim smashed back vertical and pinned against the crown. Hays, with his bushy whiskers and his slack wet mouth, I always thought looked like a dirty old man—even before I knew what a dirty old man was. I liked it when Gabby said, "Tarnation, Roy," though. My playmates and I used to say that to each other a lot. "Tarnation, Bubba Joe" and "Tarnation, Lester Ray." (Back then I even seemed to know what "tarnation" meant; now I have no idea.)

About the singing. Both Rogers and Autry felt compelled to do it, but it was something my playmates and I could take or leave alone. We viewed it sort of like we viewed Sunday school, or carrots; something that was a part our lives, but certainly not the best part. We didn't mind it exactly, but it slowed the action down. And when we showed up at the Lynn Theater there in Marshall, Texas, on our Saturday afternoons and plunked down our nine cents for the double-feature ticket, what we had come for, first and foremost, was the action. Horses galloping madly across the screen, six-shooters pop-pop-popping, bad guys biting the dust in gay profusion: oh, it was glorious, it was grand. The body count could run into the dozens within the first half hour. Few spectacles in life have been more satisfying. We used to practice dying, my playmates and I, out in our backyard. An artful, spinning, hands-to-the-chest backward tumble could sometimes gain for its performer as much approbation as the slickest cross-handed quick draw. We practiced the killing too, of course, just as intently, demanding that when someone was "shot" they have the decency to fall down. Many arguments ensued over who had shot whom, and where and when.

"Got you first."

"No, you didn't."

"Yes, I did."

And on and on.

In whose book did I recently read of a battle-weary

Marine sergeant telling a visitor to Vietnam—author Phillip Caputo, I think it was: "Before you leave here, sir, you're going to learn that one of the most brutal things in the world is your average nineteen-year-old American boy"?

Which may be why when, late in the day, Dale Evans came on the scene as Roy Rogers' distaff sidekick, slowing down the action in his movies even further, I knew I had been right all along in preferring Gene. Gene would never allow a woman to get in the way of his mayhem. A song maybe, but not a woman. Some things simply were not done. When years later in college I read Stephen Crane's marvelous (and marvelously funny) "The Bride Comes to Yellow Sky," Dale Evans was the first thing that came to mind. There it was all over again, the taming of the West—a case of, "Help me hang the curtains, dear," and Scratchy Wilson and all the other bad guys would just have to wait.

Gene and Roy, Roy and Gene. Both were genuine American success stories. The sort of too-good-to-be-true stories that still happen more often in this country than anywhere else. Gene barely had a high school education and Roy didn't even have that. Yet before they were through each man would be not only a household name but a millionaire many times over.

Gene had got his start, so the story goes, when Will Rogers came into the Frisco Railroad's telegraph office in Chelsea, Oklahoma, one evening and found the lone telegrapher, one Orvon Gene Autry, picking a guitar and singing to pass the time. Rogers supposedly listened for a while, told the young man he had talent, and suggested he take it on the radio. The year was 1927. Soon Autry was trying his luck on radio stations in New York and Chicago, imitating the leading hillbilly singer of the day, Jimmie Rogers. (Odd, all these Rogerses—Will, Jimmie, Roy—in Gene's life.) His first hit recording was "That Silver-Haired

Daddy of Mine," not a cowboy song at all, which he also helped write. It wasn't until he got out to California during the Depression that he was induced to become the first of the singing cowboys.

His first movie was *In Old Santa Fe*, starring Ken Maynard, in 1934. Autry had one scene and sang one song, but it was enough to launch him on a film career that at its height saw him turning out a new movie every six weeks. He wouldn't stop until he had made nearly a hundred of them. In addition, he was also recording songs such as "Back in the Saddle Again," which became his theme song, "Be Honest With Me" and "Mexicali Rose." In the 1950's his recordings of two children's Christmas songs, "Rudolph the Red-Nosed Reindeer" and "Here Comes Santa Claus" sold millions of copies.

For someone with his spotty background and education, Autry was a remarkably astute businessman. Over time he accumulated real estate holdings, including radio and television stations, all over Southern California. In 1982 he sold one TV station alone, Los Angeles' KTLA, for $245 million. For years he was annually listed among *Forbes* magazine's "400 Richest" Americans, right up there with the DuPonts and the Rockefellers, the Gettys and the Fords. Not bad for a country boy who started out with an eight-dollar Sears, Roebuck guitar.

And Roy Rogers? If anything, his career was even more spectacular. He had wanted to be a dentist back in Ohio because it seemed like a safe, common-sense way to make a living. But there wasn't any money for schooling so he ended up out in California picking fruit in the same Salinas Valley where Steinbeck's Joad family toiled in *The Grapes of Wrath*. A singer and square-dance caller from his youth, he helped form a trio that came to be called "The Sons of the Pioneers," and as a group they got parts in several early Westerns. His big break came in 1937 when Autry walked out on his studio, Republic Pictures, in a contract dispute and Rogers was asked to fill in for him in a film called *Under Western Skies*. Bosley Crowther, reviewing the picture in *The New York Times*, said Rogers had "a drawl like Gary Cooper" and "a smile like Shirley Temple." As with Autry, he would eventually make nearly a hundred movies. Two of his recordings with the Sons of the Pioneers, "Cool Water" and "Tumbling Tumbleweeds," would become western classics. By 1945 he was receiving 75,000 fan letters a month. A poll of the nation's schoolchildren that year placed him third behind Abraham Lincoln and Franklin Delano Roosevelt as "The American I Most Admire." Roy Rogers comic books sold millions of copies a year. More than twenty pages of the Sears catalog were devoted to Roy Rogers merchandise. At its height, before it was sold to the Marriott Corporation, the Roy Rogers restaurant chain licensed more than eight hundred franchises. When he died in 1998—the same year, coincidentally, as Autry—Rogers' personal wealth was estimated at more than $50 million.

Of the two men, Roy and Gene, Autry was said "in real life" to be much the earthier. He was known to take a drink and his language at times could be downright salty. He was also reputedly extremely tight-fisted. But then so, apparently, was Rogers, the teetotaler, the evangelical Christian. Some lessons from the Depression die hard. As Rogers liked to remind interviewers, "I hardly wore shoes until I was almost grown."

The Western has fallen out of favor in contemporary American popular culture. Its absence from today's movie and TV screens is striking. Why this should have come to pass has been a subject for debate. Some ascribe it to a national "loss of innocence" brought on by the debacle of the Viet Nam War. Others suggest that, like Tin Pan Alley, the Western just finally ran out of steam. Whatever the cause, the tipping point—almost a geological shift in its finality and abruptness—appears to have occurred sometime in the mid-1970's with the arrival on the nation's movie screens of Mel Brooks' outrageously iconoclastic *Blazing Saddles*. Where such earnest, myth-enhancing films as *Shane* and *High Noon* had defined the Western genre in the early 1950s, and *Gunsmoke* and *Bonanza* had sustained it when the Western moved to TV in the late 50's and early 60's, *Blazing Saddles*, released in 1974, left no room for doubt that times had changed. When in the film the actor and ex-NFL football star Alex Karras, as "Mongo," knocked that horse out with a single punch, he also drove a stake through the pure, beating hearts of Champion and Trigger and all they stood for. Talk about a metaphor.

As author Garry Wills has pointed out in his book *John Wayne's America*, what made the Western myth so powerful here was its pervasiveness. Since the continent was settled from the East Coast, just about everywhere in the country was at one point in our history "the west." James Fenimore Cooper's early leather-stocking hero Natty Bumppo was a westerner out there in Upstate New York. Daniel Boone was a westerner in Kentucky, Davy Crockett a westerner in Tennessee. Ohio, Iowa, Kansas, Nebraska, you name them— at one time all were out there on the Western frontier.

"America is the place where European settlers met an alien natural environment and social system," says Wills. "As the frontier moved from the Eastern Seaboard west, Americans experienced, over and over again, the excitement of the 'birth moment' when the new world was broken into, tamed, absorbed."

Even the young George Washington earned his spurs as a land surveyor out west, in western Pennsylvania.

By the time of Gene Autry and Roy Rogers—my time—the myth had undergone considerable alteration, of course. Gene and Roy weren't taming a frontier so much as they were acting out their little ninety-minute morality plays and singing us a song or two. Daniel Boone, Davy Crockett,

Kit Carson and their like never had much time for singing, or if they did the evidence of it hasn't come down to us. Autry's and Rogers' version was the Western myth at a simple, fairytale level, suitable for nine-year-old boys. As Rogers himself once put it, all his movies offered was "a little song, a little riding, a little shooting, and a girl to be saved from hazard." But the fascinating thing about Rogers and Autry both is that even as they enacted in their B-movie fashion a leached out, much-diluted version of the Western myth, they were themselves embodiments of that myth. They had both started with nothing, after all, just like the rankest of immigrants to these shores. They had re-invented themselves out of whole cloth—Rogers the Ohio farm boy more so than Autry the Panhandle Texan—, gone West, conquered their chosen territory after a long and effortful struggle, and finally, in the end, become successful and rich beyond even their own wildest imaginings. If that isn't the Western myth in a nutshell, it comes pretty close. It's what compelled the gold-rush Forty-Niners, the Donner party, the dustbowl Okies and several hundred thousand (and counting) Lana Turner and Rita Hayworth wannabes to pack their bags and head West. California is itself, and has been almost from the beginning, the goal and destination, the end point and culmination of the American myth of the West. Venice Beach and Santa Monica are where the westering impulse must finally, of necessity, come to a halt: nothing past there but blue Pacific. No more "birth moments" possible.

Nathanael West wrote a despairing little novel about Hollywood, and the whole California experience, back in the 1930's (at about the time Roy and Gene were getting their starts). He called it *The Day of the Locust*, and the title alone tells us what West thought of the place. Plague and pestilence, famine and death, a veritable apocalypse of bad outcomes was what West's little book foresaw. He had originally intended to call it *The Cheated*. It was about all the little people who came out to Hollywood and *didn't* become

Roy and Gene. As satire and sharp-edged social commentary, the novel is a gem. It still rewards re-reading. But West got it all wrong. His predictions of societal collapse, indeed of "civil war," did not hold up. History has not borne him out. Today, California is for many as alluring as it ever was, and its economy is now the seventh or eighth largest on the planet. The days of Gene and Roy, of Champion and Trigger, may be gone, but the state still acts as a magnet to those who dare to wish big. The Western itself may have disappeared from the nation's movie and TV screens, but maybe that's only because, bowing to the advances of technology, the genre has gone through a transformation and been updated. Maybe *Star Wars* is where the Western went.

Or maybe—here's an idea—*The Terminator*. That robotic, take-no-prisoners super-killer which once set in motion mows down everything in its/his path: maybe that's where the Western went.

Think about it. And think, too, about a boy growing up in a tiny, out-of-the-way village somewhere in far-off Austria. Thal, let's say, or Graz; a place not greatly unlike, in size and remoteness anyway, Gene's Tioga, Texas, or Roy's Duck Run, Ohio. Think of him watching Hollywood movies, reading American weight-lifting magazines, beginning to entertain dreams of making something of himself someday. Picture him working hard, entering some local and regional body-building contests, winning them, getting bigger, getting stronger, and eventually working his way all the way out to, yes, California. Maybe he can't sing and ride a horse. Maybe he can't even speak English without a thick accent ("Collyfornia"). But he can annihilate the bad guys, and the good guys, too! And he looks a lot better with his shirt off than Roy and Gene ever could or did.

Who knows what might happen to a boy like that? Preposterous as it sounds, he might actually make a go of it out in Hollywood, might eventually become a star of some magnitude, become fabulously wealthy, marry a Kennedy, might even end up one day as—get this—governor of the whole damn state.

Or is that too far-fetched?

www.ingramcontent.com/pod-product-compliance
Lightning Source LLC
Chambersburg PA
CBHW030637120726
47904CB00006B/2192